"YOU WANT ME AS MUCH AS I WANT YOU . . .

Don't think I haven't felt the electricity sizzling white-hot between us since we entered this hotel room," Kurt said.

Gwen blushed. Yes, she thought. It was true. Any woman would be mad not to want him. She reached up to touch a lock of his golden hair.

Their mouths locked instantly as they reached out for one another—and Gwen knew that whatever the morning might bring, she could never deny that she wanted what was going to happen this night . . .

CHARLOTTE WISELY is a writer and visual artist who spends half her time in New York City's Soho district and half her time in the solitude of her Vermont farm. She feels that writing and painting compliment each other, and she could never choose between the two. Her other Rapture Romances are *Welcome Intruder* and *Love Has No Pride*.

Dear Reader:

The editors of Rapture Romance have only one thing to say—thank you! At a time when there are so many books to choose from, you have welcomed ours with open arms, trying new authors, coming back again and again, and writing us of your enthusiasm. Frankly, we're thrilled!

In fact, the response has been so great that we feel confident that you are ready for more stories which explore all the possibilities that exist when today's men and women fall in love. We are proud to announce that we will now be publishing six titles each month, because you've told us that four Rapture Romances simply aren't enough. Of course, we won't substitute quantity for quality! We will continue to select only the finest of sensual love stories, stories in which the passionate physical expression of love is the glorious culmination of the entire experience of falling in love.

And please keep writing to us! We love to hear from our readers, and we take your comments and opinions seriously. If you have a few minutes, we would appreciate your filling out the questionnaire at the back of this book, or feel free to write us at the address below. Some of our readers have asked how they can write to their favorite authors, and we applaud their thoughtfulness. Writers need to hear from their fans, and while we cannot give out addresses, we are more than happy to forward any mail.

Happy reading!

Robin Grunder

Rapture Romance
1633 Broadway
New York, NY 10019

PASSIONATE ENTERPRISE

by
Charlotte Wisely

RAPTURE ROMANCE
NEW AMERICAN LIBRARY
TIMES MIRROR

NAL BOOKS ARE AVAILABLE AT QUANTITY DISCOUNTS
WHEN USED TO PROMOTE PRODUCTS OR SERVICES.
FOR INFORMATION PLEASE WRITE TO PREMIUM MARKETING DIVISION,
THE NEW AMERICAN LIBRARY, INC., 1633 BROADWAY,
NEW YORK, NEW YORK 10019.

SIGNET, SIGNET CLASSIC, MENTOR, PLUME, MERIDIAN AND NAL BOOKS
are published by The New American Library, Inc.,
1633 Broadway, New York, New York 10019

First Printing, December, 1983

1 2 3 4 5 6 7 8 9

PRINTED IN THE UNITED STATES OF AMERICA

Chapter One

ɞ

"Good morning, Gwen," the deep voice rang out from nowhere. "Can you come in for a minute?"

"Kurt!" Gwen looked up from her desk. "What on earth are you doing here?" she asked, before she realized how the question would sound. "I mean, yes. I'll be there in a minute."

Gwen reached up to harness the cascading brown curls that she had hastily pinned up when she stepped out of the shower that morning.

Must be something pretty special, she thought, and bent down to tuck her suede bag into the bottom drawer of her desk. She could remember only one or two other times when she had not been the first to arrive at the office. There would be no time today to recomb her hair or savor her morning cup of coffee. She got up and walked toward Kurt's office, shaking her head to jar herself awake and trying to appear alert at the same time. Although Kurt was her immediate supervisor, he wasn't the type to approach her so formally unless the situation was serious.

"This *is* a surprise," she said, her tone teasing to make up for her earlier lapse.

"Come on in," Kurt said, motioning to the leather

chair opposite him. The first rays of the morning sun pierced through the blinds and formed a grid of light and shadow on his desktop. "Rough weekend? You look a bit ragged around the edges this morning."

"Thanks a lot," she said, noticing how the sunlight also caught the highlights in his golden hair. "That's just what I need to get me started on a Monday. And what about you? Social life falling apart? You *never* make it in this early."

"As a matter of fact, my social life could stand a little improvement. . . ." Kurt began as a smile played at the corners of his mouth.

Oh no, Gwen thought. Is this really why he came in so early? To try and start something again? A momentary pause fell between them.

"Maybe I can work on it while I'm away?" he went on, and Gwen looked at him sharply.

"The Mexican project?" she asked.

Kurt nodded, his brown eyes meeting hers as his voice took on a more serious tone. "That's why I'm here at this ungodly hour. The powers that be have decided that you'll be accompanying me to Guadalajara on this trip. The computer-education units are really your baby, and they want you to help out in their presentation. Sorry to have to spring this on you so suddenly, but negotiations have been a little erratic. Do you think you can handle the job?"

"Sure," she said calmly, managing to stifle a sudden urge to jump up and down and cheer. "As a matter of fact, I've been drafting a speech for weeks. I thought you'd find my notes more useful if they were organized."

During the first month on the job Gwen had realized that unless she proved her competence by staying one step ahead in her work, she'd be stuck as a first-level administrative assistant for the next twenty years. She had taken a gamble and studied the Mexican deal on her own time.

"I've noticed you'd been giving some attention to the files." Kurt's dark eyes warmed in approval. "You'll be handling the distribution side of things. They want extensive figures on the overall profit of the venture as well as suggestions for efficient ways of marketing the units. We've already got them pretty much sold on an overall company merger, but they need help in developing a demand for the product, and a few quick lessons in general creative marketing."

He stood up and walked over to the window, pausing for a moment with his back to Gwen. Silhouetted, the contours of his rugged profile distracted her. She took a long look at the big, fair-haired man, the picture of a strong, Minnesota Viking. Most of the time, his six-foot height, chiseled features, and firm chin gave him the appearance of competence and determination. But his rather harsh features were softened by an unruly shock of bright hair that periodically fell down across his forehead. Gwen thought of her favorite childhood fairy tale about the princess who spun straw into gold. Kurt's fairness was accented by a pair of deep brown eyes that sometimes looked almost black. The contrast was startling, she thought; it seemed to reflect a paradox that lay hidden deep within him, at the core of his personality.

Gwen had known from the first moment she saw him that he was a man of action. He had an air of command that told her he went straight to the heart of any problem. Still, when she caught the mischievous expression in his eyes, she sensed that this thirty-five-year-old executive knew how to enjoy himself when he wasn't working. And she was certain that his idea of enjoyment included a beautiful companion.

"Gwen." She heard her name ring out in the familiar baritone. "Are you with me?"

"Oh, sorry," she said, thinking that she didn't function well this early in the morning. At least not before her coffee.

"As I was saying," he repeated, walking back to his desk. "I expect this will be a good opportunity for you to observe the dynamics of a complicated business arrangement."

"Absolutely," Gwen agreed emphatically. When she looked up she felt the impact of his penetrating gaze from across the desk. Her breath quickened as their eyes locked and she knew that it wasn't her sleepiness that was interfering with her clarity. My god, he's handsome, she thought, and forced herself to speak.

"I've been with Tonkan for almost a full year now, Kurt. I think I have a pretty good understanding of what's involved."

"Good," Kurt replied. "There shouldn't be any problem, then . . . his voice trailed off on a note of unresolve that Gwen felt obliged to address.

"It seems to me that we'll make a good team."

"Well, I'm glad you're so confident," Kurt replied but his tone implied that he realized, as she did, that their business relationship just wasn't that simple.

She remembered the first day she had started working at Tonkan. When she had been introduced to the rest of the staff, Kurt had seemed interested in her, and she had to admit that she had been drawn to his good looks and powerful personality. At first Gwen had tried to ignore him when he went out of his way to say hello to her, but he was persistent and she hated to keep snubbing him. Finally one night she accepted a ride home from him, and after a long day's work had even agreed to stop for a drink at a little bar on the way home. After all, they were just friends, Gwen had rationalized. They were having an innocent-enough time until Kurt had parked the car in front of her house and pulled her to him.

She couldn't deny the fact that it hadn't been easy saying no. The temptation of his strong arms, the warm pressure of his chest against her own, seemed impossible to resist. But Gwen certainly wasn't foolish enough to get involved in an office romance, especially with her boss. It would mean risking the loss of all she had worked for. She had immediately put a stop to it, and had pushed Kurt away and declared firmly that he might as well forget about starting anything with her. Kurt seemed to respect her decision, and he hadn't pursued her any further. After she became friendly with other people in the office, she learned that he was already involved with another woman. This had made her all the more relieved that she had managed to resist him. Still, there were times even now when she looked at his sensuous mouth and wondered how it would feel against her own.

When Gwen looked up she noticed that Kurt's train of thought had also wandered. His face reflected the same hungry expression it had when he had first tried to kiss her months ago. Damn! she thought. She had probably encouraged him by staring at him a few minutes before. Lusting after him is more like it, she admitted, and pulled herself up straighter in her chair.

Kurt finally looked away from her. "Let's get some coffee in here before we both go back to sleep."

"Good idea," said Gwen, and started to stand up.

"Oh, don't get up. Connie should be in by now." He reached down and pressed the buzzer on the edge of his desk. A moment later the door flew open and Kurt's secretary, Connie, stepped briskly into the room.

"Hi, Connie," Gwen said warmly. She had come to like and respect the energetic, fair-haired woman.

Kurt and Connie exchanged hellos, and then he said, "Connie, be a doll and bring us a cup of coffee. How do you take yours, Gwen?" He looked over at her.

"Oh, really, Kurt, I can get my own. Or better yet, why don't we go down to the cafeteria for coffee." She looked over at him and was greeted by a glare of annoyance.

"Honest, Gwen. I don't mind getting it," Connie assured her. She was obviously finely tuned to meet Kurt's every need.

"I really don't like the idea of being waited on," Gwen persisted. She started to renew what was a familiar argument, then she gave in and said, "Mine's regular," when she saw the pained expression on Connie's face. It wasn't fair to make Connie a bone of contention when she was standing right there.

As soon as Connie was out of the room, Gwen reopened the conversation. "You know, Kurt," she said, "Connie is a bright woman who has talents far beyond making coffee and taking shorthand."

"You don't say," Kurt replied disinterestedly.

"As a matter of fact," Gwen went on doggedly, "I think she's one of the smartest employees we have, and shouldn't be playing nursemaid to you or to anyone else here."

"Please, Gwen, no feminist sermons this morning." Kurt frowned. "It's not as if I think of Connie as my servant. It's just that it's not to the benefit of Tonkan for me to waste my time making coffee and running errands. Someone's got to do it, and that's part of what these girls are hired for in the first place."

"Women, Kurt *women*," Gwen said quickly. "And I suppose that you also think that the most important qualification for a woman is a high score on the typing test?"

"And just what, exactly, is wrong with that?" Kurt asked.

"What's wrong with that is that women are not machines." Gwen suddenly let her irritation unfurl. "We're human beings who should be given a chance to use our brains and develop our potential."

When Kurt looked unaffected by her words, Gwen decided to change her strategy and deliver a more personal blow. "Why, I bet that with time and proper training, Connie could easily handle your job . . . she might even do it better."

"That's ridiculous," Kurt said, and for a brief second Gwen thought she had hit a nerve.

As she watched a closed expression come over his face she became aware of the muffled sounds of the office as it came to life outside the room; an announcement of the busy day that lay ahead of her. She knew that she could sit there forever, arguing with Kurt, and probably get nowhere. She might as well retreat and retrench. "And to think that all this time I was hoping that your male chauvinist conditioning was weakening," she said with a heartfelt sigh.

An expression of guilt swept quickly across Kurt's face, but instead of defending himself, he pulled up to the edge of the desk and, peering over at her, asked, "Does this mean that our relationship is over?" He managed to look contrite, sincere, and sexy all at once.

Gwen was disarmed by his charm and for a moment could find no words to express her frustration without sounding stuffy. How clever he was at manipulating conversation, she thought.

"What it means is that I think I'll take my coffee and drink it at my own desk." She stood up and said "Thanks" as Connie handed her the cup.

As she walked toward the door, she turned around to Kurt and said, "I'll come back later to discuss the merger." There was still an edge to her voice.

But Gwen couldn't help but smile when she heard him mutter, "I'm going to have to listen to this all the way to Mexico. . . ."

Chapter Two

❧

"I'm so excited for you," Betty said earnestly three days later as she sat on the edge of Gwen's bed and watched her pack. "I've always dreamed of going to Mexico. Isn't there a little corner of that suitcase that you could tuck me into? I'd hold my breath all the way to Guadalajara."

"Oh, Betty." Gwen laughed. "I wish you could come with me too. If I'd been given more notice, we might have been able to arrange for you to join me after the meetings. Definitely, let's plan on doing that the next time." Although they were almost the same size, she had always seen Betty, with her lanky frame, straight red hair, and inquisitive blue eyes, as her physical opposite. Instead of beauty, Betty's looks reflected intelligence and an insatiable curiosity about everyone she met. It had been Betty, who was studying anthropology at the University of Minnesota and had needed a quiet place, who initially discovered the large apartment in the old, four-story house that sat perched on the edge of a tree-lined street not far from the lake. And it had been Betty who had initiated their first, rather bizarre encounter.

Gwen remembered vividly the night they had

16

met at the party of a mutual friend. She had been sitting with a group of people on the floor in front of Betty when the redheaded girl had reached down and accidentally rubbed her hand across the top of Gwen's head.

"A keel!" Betty had shouted, oblivious to everyone's stares. "As far as we know, only the Eskimos consistently have keels," Betty, the anthropologist, explained later, pointing to the subtle ridge that ran along the top of Gwen's skull.

"That means that either I've drifted a long way from home or else I'm a freak," Gwen had responded, sparking a long conversation that led to their present friendship.

Betty reached out and tucked the corner of a blouse back into the suitcase. "At least we know you'll be in good company, what with Kurt Jensen escorting you around. What a hunk! And to think that you'll be seeing him every day. How will you ever be able to control yourself?"

"Believe me, I'll manage," was Gwen's terse reply. She carefully folded a pair of white dungarees and laid them out as flat as she could over the bright-pink cotton shirt that completed the outfit.

"You're honestly going to sit there and tell me you have absolutely no interest in Kurt Jensen?" Betty seemed genuinely astonished.

"Of course not. You'd have to be blind not to be attracted to Kurt. And he's also intelligent and can be a lot of fun. But as much as he thinks he's liberated, Kurt is one of those conceited, chauvinistic types who couldn't survive being with a strong woman for a minute. Do you know that he actually has Connie, his secretary, running errands and serving him coffee?"

"You're kidding!" Betty responded with mock horror.

"No, I'm not," Gwen said, and dropped the lid on the suitcase to make sure it would still close. "With his attitude, I doubt if Kurt and I will ever see eye to eye. I'll be lucky if we can keep from fighting during the trip."

"Still," Betty said with a far-away look in her eyes, "It's a shame to see someone like him go to waste. Maybe he just needs to be educated, Gwen. A few good arguments with you along with a couple of books and he might just wake up and see the light."

"I don't know, Betty." Gwen looked over at her friend with sudden seriousness. "It's not my mission in life to go around trying to change people. And besides that, Kurt's good looks and all of his other good qualities, he could probably have any woman he wants."

"That may be so," Betty's voice trailed off as she left the room and in a moment returned. "But they'll all pale beside you in this creation," she said, holding up her new, never-worn red chiffon dress.

"Oh, Betty. I couldn't," said Gwen, overwhelmed by her friend's kind gesture. The shimmering, silky dress was cut in a crisscross style across the bodice so that it left absolutely nothing to the imagination. And the calf-length skirt was long and flowing, made to hug the figure and reveal every curve. Gwen knew that it would fit because she had tried it on when Betty was deciding whether or not to buy it, and the feeling of the soft material against her skin and the reflection of the sophisticated stranger in the dressing-room mirror had made her feel light-headed and beautiful.

"Betty, are you sure you want me to take it? After all, you've never even worn it."

"I insist that you take it," Betty said, "with my love. I ask only that you *try* not to spill anything on it, and that when you do wear it you have a wonderful time. And remember, a dress like this is not made to be worn for long. This, my friend, is designed to be taken off . . . preferably by Kurt."

A little embarrassed, Gwen gave Betty a thank-you hug. "Thanks a million for the dress. I promise you I'll try and wear it well. But as for how long . . ." The two friends broke into laughter.

Gwen quickly finished her packing, and then spent a restless night tossing and turning in bed, thinking about the coming trip. This was her chance to really shine, and in spite of what she had said to Betty, it was Kurt who had given her this opportunity. She couldn't fail—for his sake and hers.

The next thing she knew, it was morning, and she was making her last-minute preparations, hoping all the time that she had remembered to bring everything she needed. It wasn't till she was settled in the cab, looking out the window at the beautiful spring day, that her jitters returned. She gave the driver a handsome tip after he pulled up in front of the Tonkan building and helped her with her luggage. She accepted his hearty thanks as a kind of good omen for the rest of the day, and feeling lighthearted and even a little excited, she punched the button on the elevator that would take her to the seventh floor.

I hope I'm going to be able to handle these, she thought, and lugged the heavy suitcases over to her desk. She was startled when she looked up and saw Kurt standing in the doorway watching her.

"Hello!" She smiled, and wondered what had gotten him up this early on yet another morning.

"Hello, yourself," he said. "*I've* already made the coffee. Won't you come in?"

As she brushed past him into his office Gwen noticed the faint shadow of beard around his chin and thought to herself that today it was Kurt who looked as if he had just crawled out of bed—or, probably more accurately, had never been *in* bed.

"There's been a slight hitch in plans," he said, taking a precarious perch on the edge of his desk after Gwen had seated herself in the leather chair. They were sitting closer together than she might have preferred. "Connie was called home unexpectedly by a sudden death in her family, so she won't be coming with us. Fortunately for us," he went on, "she's already taken care of reservations, meeting schedules, and details like that. But on trips like this, I rely heavily on Connie to handle both the paperwork and any incidental clerical duties. It's too late to call in someone else. I'm afraid, Gwen, that I'm just going to have to ask you to step in and take over for her."

Gwen caught herself just as her mouth was about to fall open in surprise. She made an effort to control her sudden urge to tell Kurt *exactly* what she thought of his plan that she replace Connie, but somehow, miraculously, when she began to speak, her voice was calm and rational. "Poor Connie! Well, we'll just have to make the best of things. It's really too bad—normally I'd be happy to substitute for Connie—but of course that's impossible. I'll be too busy with the presentation. But I'm sure that if I call ahead, it will be no problem getting a temporary secretary in Mexico. In fact, we can probably even find one who's bilingual!" She spoke with the assurance of an experienced organizer.

"Right," Kurt said immediately, looking almost stunned by her show of efficiency. But it seemed to escape his notice that his plan had been, for her, demeaning.

They were leaving immediately after lunch, so Gwen hurried back to her desk, made the call to Mexico, and spent the next couple of hours cleaning up all of the business that had to be taken care of before leaving. By the time they were ready to go, she was caught up in double-checking the last-minute details, but even in the midst of the flurry of activity, she was beginning to feel slightly nervous. It was only recently that she had admitted to herself that she was, in fact, frightened of flying. It was mild phobia, she rationalized, but real enough to make her palms sweat in the boarding lines before takeoff.

"We've got to hurry." Kurt was suddenly standing beside her, and Gwen grabbed for her things, took a deep breath, and bid a silent farewell to her comfortable little niche at Tonkan.

Once they were down on the street, hailing a

cab, Gwen began to feel better. Kurt's "to the airport" sounded like music to her ears, and she realized that it was probably the waiting that had been making her tense. Now, finally, they were on their way.

Kurt rolled down his window a crack and Gwen felt a current of cool air gently slap her face. "Is that too much breeze for you?" he asked.

"No. It feels good." She exhaled a long sigh of relief. "I'm glad we finally got out of there," she said, and drew her hands across her lap to smooth down her skirt. Gwen knew that she looked attractive in the expensive linen suit with slightly padded shoulders that brought a fashionable, 1930s look to the costume. The moss-green silk blouse she wore underneath picked up the subtle green threads of the linen and accentuated her smooth, ivory complexion.

Kurt also seemed to be settling down beside her. As he drew up his hand and raked his fingers through his ruffled hair, Gwen looked over at him, captivated by the simple gesture. What exactly was it about him that fascinated her so? she wondered. She shifted her legs slightly to avoid any contact.

"I guess these papers could use a going-over before we get there." Kurt reached for a file folder from out of his briefcase. "The head of the company is a man named Phanor. Fully in favor of the deal, I'm told."

"That's great," Gwen exclaimed happily, and reached for the report. She mustn't let her mind wander from the business at hand. After all, there was so much to learn on this trip.

"You really do like your work, don't you?" Kurt asked suddenly, as if the realization had just hit him.

"Of course," she replied quickly, irritated by the patronizing ring of the remark. "Why else would I be putting in twelve-hour days at Tonkan?"

"Well, I couldn't ask for a more enthusiastic—or better-looking—partner," Kurt said, falling back into his usual habit of avoiding a question he didn't want to answer. Someday she would point this out to him, she thought, and said, "Thanks for the compliment—not that my looks should make any difference. *Qualified* may be the word you're looking for." The assurance in her voice left no room for argument, and the conversation came to a halt along with the cab when they reached the noisy, congested metropolitan airport.

Once there, Kurt quickly took over and moved them both neatly out of the cab, through the check-in line, and into the waiting area. When they finally stood in the boarding line and watched as the passengers ahead of them began to disappear into the belly of the shiny, metallic aircraft, Kurt looked over at her and said, "Having the last-minute jangles?"

"Oh, not really," she lied, and tried to look as composed as she possibly could. Wouldn't it be easier to just admit that I'm afraid of airplanes, she asked herself, instead of being so stoic about it all? A little neurosis over flying certainly isn't going to influence his opinion of me.

When Gwen asked to take the aisle seat, wanting to have quick access to the ladies' room, she thought she had given herself away, but Kurt simply settled in and spread out his papers before him. The takeoff was smooth, and when the plane broke through the thin layer of clouds that from the ground had blocked out the bright spring sun, Gwen gasped at the magnificence of the sight. They had risen up into a golden light that offered freshness and clarity and brought a sheen to the silvery wing of the giant bird.

By the time the plane had leveled off and the "No Smoking" sign in the front of the cabin had been turned off, Gwen was finally beginning to relax. She stretched her legs a little, and when she reached for the armrest her elbow accidentally made contact with Kurt's arm. This fleeting touch was enough to break his concentration, and he turned his head and looked over at her.

"Well," he said, "it looks like we made it."

"Thank heavens," she replied, and managed a weak smile.

"Gwen! Are you afraid of flying?" He looked as if he was going to rib her, but his smile faded when she showed him the worry in her eyes.

"To be honest, yes," she confided. "I don't know why or how it started, but every time I step on a plane I feel as if I'm going up for good. Silly, isn't it?" She looked down to hide her embarrassment.

"No. Not really. In fact"—he reached out and folded her icy fingers in his warm hand—"when you stop to think about it, there are a lot of reasons to be afraid of flying." Gwen shot him a grateful smile that urged him to go on. His low voice was comforting, and she could feel her taut nerves begin to unwind.

"I've always thought that Icarus was a relentless compulsive who thought he was immortal and that the Wright brothers were two machos in it for the glory. None of them stopped to consider the side effects of flying on us poor land lovers who don't like their gravity pulled out from under them." Kurt stopped speaking and looked over at her. "What do you think?"

"Mmmm, what?" Gwen was jarred back to reality by the sudden silence. His voice was so soothing that she had let herself drift away into the gauzy cloud formations that floated outside the window. "I'm sorry. I guess I wasn't listening." She laughed lightly. "But whatever you said really did the trick. I feel fine now, Kurt. I'm just going to powder my nose, and then maybe we can try and work."

Gwen stood up and made her way to the washroom in the rear of the plane. She felt even better after she had splashed her face with cool water and freshened up her makeup. As she eased her way back up the aisle she felt miraculously cured of all her earlier anxiety.

Then, the plane lurched. Gwen still hadn't settled herself into her seat, and the sudden motion cast her forward. Kurt reacted instantly, reaching up to break her fall. Gwen felt the shock of his sudden nearness, realizing that his face was now just inches from her own. For a brief second, she was held captive by his closeness and could not move.

"I'm sorry," she said at last when she came to her senses and pulled herself upright.

"My pleasure," Kurt replied, and Gwen feigned

an expression of annoyance in response to his seductive smile.

"Let's get to work," she said, and reached for the case under her seat. Between the papers Kurt had given her to read over and trying to find something edible in what could only be called an attempt at a meal, the rest of the flight passed quickly. Gwen could hardly believe it when she heard the captain's voice announce their impending landing.

She gripped the arms of her chair in an effort to steel herself for the fall, and then felt the warmth of Kurt's protective hand as it covered her own.

"Easy does it," he soothed. All through the descent he held her hand, his touch a lifeline of strength that held her until they felt the bump of the plane's touchdown.

They stepped off the plane, entered a world that was vivid with color, and were greeted by the sweet perfume of the bougainvillea that grew everywhere. Kurt took Gwen's elbow and steered her through the crowds, and in no time they had collected their luggage and were once again on their way.

"*Buenos días*," said the man at the entrance of the airport. Gwen answered in her best accent, glad that she had taken time to brush up a little on her Spanish. Kurt, however, was fluent, and within minutes he had them situated in a cab, heading for the hotel.

"For better or for worse," she heard him say, and she wrenched her attention away from the paradise around them to look at him, "Mexican culture has been strongly affected by the United

States. In some areas you would think you were in parts of California. I think it's for worse—I've always liked the grandeur of the original Spanish influence, and though it's more rare, the imprint of the initial inhabitors, the Indians. If you look hard, you'll notice touches of Aztec style here and there. Funny, isn't it," he went on, for once seeming completely sincere, "me talking like this and at the same time trying to sell the Mexicans computers? But, of course, it does make sense when you think that it is simply a way of using modern technology to teach people their real history, to help them hang on to their roots."

Gwen listened attentively to his musings without comment.

"Another thing about Mexico, Gwen. I think I'd better warn you about the men here. They really go for American women, and they're apt to be pretty aggressive, so be careful who you get friendly with."

Gwen put her hand to her mouth to stifle a giggle. Kurt was so serious about his advice, so protective. "I appreciate your concern," she said, trying not to make him angry. "But I've had lots of experience dealing with men like that right in my own back yard. I think I'll be able to handle that Mexican brand of chauvinism."

Kurt arched a quizzical eyebrow and stared down at her, and Gwen smiled. She could see that she had gotten through to him, and had given him something to think about.

When they pulled up to an older, Spanish-style hotel that seemed to be a bit removed from the main drag, Gwen wasn't surprised by Kurt's choice, after what he had just been saying. Nor did she have any doubt that in addition to being picturesque, it was among the most elegant hotels in the city. Kurt liked to travel in style.

As they entered the main lobby Gwen gasped at the thousands of intricately designed mosaic tiles that adorned its walls. From where they were standing she caught a glimpse of the large, central courtyard that overflowed with bright, exotic blossoms, lacy green foliage, and colorful birds. Lost in the beauty of her surroundings, she paid no attention to Kurt's discussion with the desk clerk.

"Unfortunately," Kurt replied after a short consultation with the desk clerk, "the wrong reservation was canceled and you've been assigned to what would have been Connie's room. I'm afraid that our rooms are connected to the same suite, but I assure you that they are as separate as two rooms could ever be. I was not planning to seduce you—at least not by such underhanded means.

"Oh, don't worry about me," Gwen said flippantly. Their close proximity was nothing she couldn't handle, she reassured herself as they stepped into the corridor. But in the next instant she began to wonder as she and Kurt found themselves again in the midst of a throng of people who all insisted on squeezing into the elevator. She could feel his hard thighs pressed against her, his warm breath ruffling her hair. When the door finally opened, it was not a moment too soon for her self-control.

If Gwen had been going to complain about the

suite, she was glad she had not done so. It was splendid. The sparsely furnished room was painted in pastel colors that accented its elegant Spanish lines. Double doors opened out onto a balcony that overlooked the city of Guadalajara. Gwen gasped when she stepped out to have a look.

"It's magnificent, isn't it?" She heard his voice at her elbow.

"Unbelievable," she answered, and was startled to find that he was looking at her and not at the view.

"You still look tired, Gwen. Jet lag. I think it would do us both good to have a little nap before dinner."

"Yes," she responded reluctantly, "I guess so," and wondered, did she really need sleep at a time like this? Still, he was the more experienced traveler, and had been right about everything so far.

Two hours later Gwen was awakened from a sound sleep by a light tapping on her door. She jumped up and out of bed and reached for her soft yellow robe. When she opened her door and looked out, she found Kurt peering in at her with a still-sleepy look in his eyes. "Hungry?" he asked, and moved a step closer.

"Starving," she responded, and smiled up at him.

His glance fell to the soft swell of flesh that was exposed by her open robe. But he quickly averted his eyes and said, "Let's eat, then."

Exactly half an hour later Gwen appeared at the entrance to the dining room feeling fresh and clean—and extremely hungry. She had dressed quickly so that she wouldn't keep Kurt waiting, deciding to forgo formality and wear a simple, flowered cotton sundress with her white sandals. She pinned up her hair in a casual way so that several tiny ringlets, still wet from her bath, encircled her face like a garland of little flowers and gave her a regal air. Her cheeks shone rosy red and the freshness and vitality she radiated caused heads to turn as she entered the room.

"Gwen," Kurt said and rose to greet her. "I know I should tell you your promptness is the sign of a good businessperson, but I'd rather tell you you're beautiful. Here, have this chair—you'll be able to look out into the garden. Like a tropical jungle, isn't it?"

Gwen settled herself at the table. "Yes. I feel as if I'm in another world," she said, ignoring his comment although she knew she was blushing. *Damn* his charm. But her attention was quickly diverted when she noticed how Kurt's beige sports suit and light blue shirt set off his golden good looks and how the dappled shadows emphasized the rugged angularity of his features.

Gwen let Kurt order the meal, and was not disappointed. He rattled off names of dish after dish and before long every inch of the table was covered with colorful, exotic Mexican specialties. They sipped margaritas as they slowly began to make inroads in the many plates of food.

"Gwen," Kurt said when the waiter brought yet another platter heaped with several different versions of the typical Mexican taco, enchilada, tostado, and burrito, "do you realize that we've never actually sat down and talked before? And we've been working together for a long time now."

"That's true," said Gwen absentmindedly, trying to decide where to begin eating.

"I'd like to know a little bit about where you grew up, and how you wound up at Tonkan in the first place."

"Kurt"—Gwen laughed—"The way you put it, I almost feel as if I'm being interviewed."

"I'm sorry," he said quickly. She realized too late that she had embarrassed him a little.

'Oh, Kurt, I was just kidding," she said gently. "You should know by now that I *always* like talking about myself." She took a good-sized bite of cheese enchilada before she began. "I grew up in the town of Mankato. I'm sure you've heard of it. It's an hour or so from south of Minneapolis, near the teachers' college—you know the one I mean. As a kid I loved it. I always thought of myself as roughing it in the country; I'd pretend I was Laura Ingalls Wilder. It's only now that I've moved away that I realize it was quite sophisticated for a town its size."

Kurt nodded his head, encouraging her to go on. Strange, she thought, I never would have imagined that Kurt, the office playboy, would be interested in childhood reminiscences.

She continued. "I guess there was nothing too special about my childhood. Oh, I was the baby of the family; my mother was almost forty when she had me, so I got lots of attention from my parents. Dwight, my brother, and Nan, my older sister, were already on their way up when I came along.

I guess I was doted on by them all—and I loved every minute of it."

"Sounds nice," Kurt said, his dark eyes fixed intently on her, drawing her out to reveal more than the bare bones of her life. *It's as if,* she thought, *he wants to know everything about me, even my darkest secrets.*

"As a child I liked math, science, and what used to be considered 'boys' things,' and I was good at them. At first Mom had trouble understanding, but she came around and even encouraged me. I would trail after my brother Dwight— he's a chemist now—and even watch while he did his homework. He didn't mind and would talk to me about what he was doing. But"—she raised a finger into the air—"I *did* have one doll, who went everywhere with me."

Kurt laughed softly at the image, and then asked, "What did your father do?"

"Oh, he ran a small business in town. Nothing spectacular." Gwen said, "but somehow we always had just enough money to get by. And when things got tight, we'd all go out and take little jobs to make ends meet. Dad was raised on the farm himself, and he was never highly motivated to go after the mighty dollar, or to give up the simple things in life that he enjoyed so much. I never for a moment felt deprived of anything as a child. We had so much fun. Raising all kinds of animals, keeping a huge garden, going out exploring all over the area. I was even a member of 4-H, and once I won a blue ribbon at the county fair. . . ."

As she talked Gwen felt herself drifting off, back into her past, and she stopped for a moment to try and relocate herself in the present. It took only one look at the sensuous fullness of Kurt's lips as he smiled to jolt her back to reality.

"I'd like to meet your folks someday." Kurt said, and somehow Gwen knew he wasn't just being polite.

"Oh," she said, looking down at her plate. "They're both dead now."

"I'm sorry." He reached across the table and took her hand, sending shivers up her arm. The gesture, meant as comfort, became something more, something that Gwen knew they had both felt. After a silent moment, he released her hand.

"It's okay, Kurt," she said shakily, her voice belying her words. She went on, wanting to reassure him but knowing that she could tell him what she had never freely discussed with anyone before. "It happened a long time ago, about the time I was starting college. They had decided to make a trip up north to look at some land. "Funny," she said as she put down her fork, "initially Mom didn't want to go, but Dad managed to talk her into it. Anyway, they were coming back late at night, along a narrow road, when a drunk joyrider lost control and crashed into them. I guess Dad couldn't move fast enough to get out of the way . . . everyone was killed.

"But I've still got Dwight and Nan." Gwen smiled broadly, and a wave of warmth put her in touch with all of the love she felt for them. "After the accident, we were together all the time, trying to work out the loss, and to move ahead together. We knew my folks wouldn't have wanted us to mourn for long; they lived a full and happy life, and wanted the same for their children. Both Nan and Dwight still live upstate. Nan's a pediatrician. She has so much positive energy that she can almost cure kids by just looking at them."

Kurt looked down at his hands, clasped in front of him, and she wondered what he was thinking. "You all sound so tight-knit and supportive," he finally said wistfully.

"Oh, that's for sure," Gwen said, and put her napkin down alongside her plate. It was time to change the subject, she thought. Too much of anyone's family could get boring. "I'm stuffed. The meal was absolutely delicious."

"Yes, wasn't it?" Kurt said, but he still looked as if he was far away, lost in the story she had just told him. "Waiter." He finally seemed to snap out of it. "We'll have our coffee now," he said. Gwen was glad when the empty plates were removed from the table and she didn't have to be reminded of how much they had eaten.

"Tell me about what's going to happen tomorrow," she said after the coffee arrived.

"Well," Kurt answered, "we plan to start the meetings tomorrow morning." He took a sip of the hot, steaming *café con leche*. "Phanor, the Mexican representative, is coming here with his entourage. There's a good-sized conference room at the hotel, so we decided that there was no need to go elsewhere."

Gwen nodded in agreement.

"We'll have three long, all-day sessions with the Mexican representatives. Everyone agreed that it would be better to do it that way instead of drawing out the meetings over a longer period. We'll probably even work through siesta."

"I agree," Gwen replied. "The best approach is a straightforward, concise presentation of our proposal. As beautiful as it is here, we could become spoiled if we were to stay too long." She took another look around the fantasylike room, imagining, before she could stop herself, what it would be like to be here with Kurt when neither of them had any businesslike facade to maintain.

By the time the meal was over, Gwen was heady from the surroundings, the margaritas . . . and Kurt's company, a tiny voice whispered. She ignored it and walked out of the restaurant alongside Kurt in a daze, trying to resist the temptation to take his arm or lean against him. And when the elevator came to a halt and she started toward the suite, she was all too aware of his presence behind her.

"Why don't you join me in my room for a nightcap?" he urged. "We'll leave the door open." He said it jokingly, but she knew that what was happening between them was all too serious.

Common sense told Gwen to say no. But the powerful charm behind Kurt's sweet smile was too much for her to resist. "Okay," she said lightly, trying to conceal her nervousness, "one drink."

She walked into Kurt's room and was intoxicated by the delicious smell of flowers that grew far below his balcony window. All of her senses seemed heightened in Mexico. She turned to accept that drink that he offered her and their fingers brushed.

"To the merger," he said, and stepped toward her with a raised hand.

"To the merger," Gwen echoed. When their glasses touched, their eyes also met and locked in a long, intimate exchange.

"Gwen." Kurt simply said her name, and then put his glass down and moved toward her. He grasped her arms, pulled her to him, and brought his lips down on her mouth. Any resistance Gwen had been planning, any doubts she still felt, fled the moment he touched her. The softness of his lips, the feeling of his strong chest against her breasts, caused shivers of delight to ripple through her body. There *was* something special between them; she had felt it while they talked. This was nothing like that other time. . . .

Kurt's arms tightened around her, his insistent tongue darted into her mouth in search of acceptance, and she answered him in the unspoken language of desire.

"Gwen, I want you," he said thickly after he finally broke their kiss.

"I'm not sure I know what I'm doing." Gwen looked into his eyes as a sudden wave of confusion swept over her. The intensity of the passion she saw there made her almost afraid.

"You know what you're doing," he said firmly, "and you want me as much as I want you." He bent down and kissed her again, quickly, sweetly, and then laughed and said, "Don't think I don't feel the electricity that's been sizzling white hot between us—since we walked into this room."

Gwen blushed hotly. Yes, she thought. It was probably true. Any woman would be mad not to want him. She reached up to touch a lock of his golden hair.

In a swift movement that took her by surprise, Kurt bent down, picked her up, and carried her to the bed. He put her down gently, then lay beside her, and their mouths locked instantly as they reached out for one another. Kurt's lips left her mouth and lowered for a taste of her milky breast, as her hands found their way up and under his shirt, to begin a journey that would take her down his broad shoulders to the muscular ridges of his back, and finally to the inward slopes of his narrow hips.

"I want to look at you," Kurt murmured, and began to undress her. "Let me do it," he insisted when she tried to help, and piece by piece he discarded her clothing and drank in the beauty of every inch of her smooth, white body.

"If you knew how often I've pictured you like this." He quickly shed his own clothing, till he stood before her unclothed. Gwen muffled her own joyful cry at the magnificent sight of him.

"Oh, Kurt." She sighed as the weight of his body settling next to her formed a warm nest in the bed and pulled them together into its softness. The feeling of his skin, naked against her own, enflamed her entire body.

Kurt took his hand and ran it slowly, slowly, the length of her body. His light brown skin was slightly rough, the color and texture of finely sanded wood, and his musky taste and smell brought visions of the damp, wet earth after a heavy rainfall. Quivering with passion, she began her own teasing, barely perceptible exploration.

"Don't stop," Kurt whispered to her, and she sighed and braved the long voyage down, down to the heart of his manhood. Far more than anything more direct or demanding, her sensitive touch aroused him. He lowered his mouth to make a sensuous flight across her stomach and thighs, and then restraint was gone as their gentle caresses became a frenzied mutual possession. In a wild burst of desire they came together, set sail and soared higher and higher, as if caught in a strong wind that flung them forward toward a heavenly destination. But Kurt was strong; and he wanted them to arrive together. For a few moments he moved slowly, and they were becalmed and rocking, rocking in a docile current. Then, as he heard Gwen's soft cries, felt her telltale quivers, he let the wind rise high again. It swept through the room, and sent them reeling on a swift, savage path toward the sun. At the last moment, when rapture was so exquisite she feared she could bear no more, she felt herself exploding on a crest of fulfillment and pleasure that freed her from the earth itself, no longer mortal flesh but pure joy.

Afterward they lay back, folded in one another's arms, while Kurt let his fingers roam through her thick, dark hair. Gwen felt relaxed and peaceful, glad that she had decided to stay with him, sure her instincts had been right.

After a while though, a nagging thought disturbed her voluptuous tranquility. "Kurt," she said, running a hand up and down his muscular arm, "we're going to have to be careful. You know the way they are at Tonkan."

"I know," he said, and she was glad to see that

he was taking her seriously. "We'll just have to practice a little discretion," he decided.

"You don't mind, then, if I go back to my own room to sleep tonight?" she asked timidly. As much as she wanted to stay with him, she felt exposed and vulnerable lying with him in a hotel room while they were on a business trip, as if her co-workers at Tonkan were actually watching them. If she and Kurt were going to be lovers, it would take awhile to get used to it.

Kurt sat up in bed beside her and took her face gently in his hands. He brought his mouth to hers in a long, good-night kiss. "I'll miss you tonight," he whispered, "but I understand. You run along to your room now and get a good night's sleep. I'll see you in the morning." He gave her a quick hug.

Gwen got up and started to leave, but turned on impulse to throw him one last kiss.

"And Gwen," he called after her, "don't worry about what others might say. What happens between us is strictly our business."

Chapter Three

When she opened her eyes, the first thing Gwen noticed was her room's fresco. She lay in bed motionless, admiring the pale pink and blue hues of the faded design that bordered the edges of the high walls and ceiling. The entire room was bathed in bright-yellow sunlight that poured in through the open slats in the blinds that she had forgotten to pull the night before.

The first thing she thought of, as she instinctively reached out and turned the face of her travel clock toward her to check the time, was Kurt. The memory of the night before came rushing back, and she felt a pang of excitement, knowing that in a few moments she would see him.

Dismissing any thoughts of further sleep, Gwen got up and walked out onto the balcony to drink in the splendor of the city. On the street below people were gearing up for the day's work, and smells of breakfast wafted up to greet her, arousing her appetite. She was glad that the shower turned out to be of the present decade, even if the hotel itself was not. The sharp, hot needles of water beat down on her and sifted out the sluggish residue of sleep, so that when she was finally wrapped in a thick white towel, ready to select the day's outfit, she was alert and wide-awake. Stop daydreaming about your lover, she told herself mock scoldingly, and start thinking about your career.

Gwen chose her clothes carefully, knowing how important it was to make the right kind of appearance at the first meeting. She had to dress formally, and look somewhat reserved. Still, Mexico was the land of sun, a passionate country that expressed itself with bright color. She picked out a soft turquoise blouse with a pleated front and round neck to wear under her dove-gray, raw silk suit. And when she slipped on a coral and turquoise bracelet and earrings to match, she knew that she had found just the right accessories.

By the time she was dressed, Gwen was so hungry that she almost forgot about her jitters over the upcoming meeting. But when she grabbed her briefcase and took one last look around the room to make sure she hadn't forgotten anything, she felt the bones in her legs turn to jelly. She wondered if the hollow in her stomach wasn't due to anxiety after all—and if the anxiety was entirely due to the business meeting ahead of her. She took a deep breath before she swung out the door, reminding herself that, above all else, she must remain calm.

"*Buenos días*," she said to the host as she walked into the dining room, and then flinched at the sound of her imperfect accent. Boy, did her Spanish need work!

" 'Ello," came his barely recognizable reply. Touché, Gwen thought, and immediately felt better.

By the time he had seated her at a charming table in the middle of the outdoor courtyard, she had learned that his name was Ramón and that he was responsible for taking care of her during her stay at the Campo Bello. She smiled up at him gratefully as he handed her the menu, then started to study it carefully.

"*Juevos rancheros y café con leche,*" she heard someone say, and when she raised her eyes over the menu she saw Kurt pulling out the chair across from her.

"Good morning," she said with a shy smile.

"Hi there, gorgeous." He returned her smile with a look of smoldering sensuality that made her wish the day were already over and their night together about to begin, then picked up his napkin and adjusted himself in the white, wrought-iron chair that was a little too small for his large frame. He reached out, and with a movement too quick for a casual observer to notice, caressed the pulse point of her wrist, sending a rush of sensation through her. His blond hair was still damp from the shower, so that the undisciplined shock that usually fell down across his forehead was plastered back, exposing his strong temples. Gwen noticed that the coffee–brown shirt under his lightweight beige suit called attention to his dark eyes and brought a touch of drama and intensity to his overall appearance. If I didn't already feel what I feel for him—she didn't let herself analyze what that feeling was—I'd be feeling it now, Gwen thought.

"Yes, I think I'll have the *juevos rancheros.* Why don't you try it, Gwen? It's the Mexican way of cooking eggs with hot pepper, to get you going, *pronto.*"

Gwen smiled over at him and agreed, and once her meal arrived, she found herself gobbling it up with relish, even though normally she didn't even eat breakfast. As they ate, Kurt told Gwen about his past experiences in Mexico. From the humorous stories over misunderstandings about language to his sensitive descriptions of visits to the Mayan ruins, Gwen was captivated. But as they sipped their *café con leche* and he continued on, she couldn't help but think that it was not only what he was saying that captured her attention. It was his energy, the fluid sensitivity of his face as it reflected his emotions, and the depth of conviction he showed when he talked about what was deeply important to him. And behind it lay the precious memory of their intimate night together.

The mood changed quickly, though, when he glanced down at his watch and exclaimed, "My god! Look at the time." All thoughts turned to the business at hand, and after signing for the meal, Kurt and Gwen rushed off to the conference room on the second floor.

Gwen stepped into the conference room and immediately saw that it, too, was another architectural wonder. It was large and airy, with high latticed windows that again opened onto balconies that hung out over the street. She could see that there had been an attempt at simplicity in the decor of the room; it was painted white with no other adornments. The long table that ran its length looked from a distance like a part of a stage set: simple, serviceable, and appropriate for business.

As soon as they entered, a short, black-haired man stood up and walked toward them with an outstretched hand. Kurt stepped forward and extended his own hand to the gentleman before Gwen could react. "Good morning," he said. "I'm Kurt Jensen."

"Juan Pablo de Phanor," came the reply, and Gwen knew that this was the president of Productos Mexicanos, the person who would make the ultimate decision regarding the merger.

"I'd like you to meet Gwen Franklin," Kurt said, and Gwen also shook his hand. "How do you do," she said smiling. "I'm pleased to meet you."

"Please," came his reply, "call me Juan. Come and meet the rest of our group." He placed his hand lightly on Gwen's elbow and steered her to the table, leaving Kurt to follow. "First, this is my daughter, Arzelia," he said, and gestured toward a woman sitting to his right.

When she turned her head to say hello, Gwen saw that she was stunningly beautiful. But even as she greeted Gwen, her eyes wandered over to Kurt.

After brief introductions to the other five men, everyone sat down. When Gwen looked around after settling herself in her chair and arranging her papers in front of her, she saw that several of the others were looking at her. She wasn't sure what Arzelia's function was at the meeting, but it was soon clear from her informal, rather indifferent demeanor that she would not be playing a key role in the negotiations.

When Phanor finally called the meeting to order, Gwen experienced a moment of cold fear. She knew that Mexican men had no reputation for encouraging independence in their women, and the question occurred to her, will they even listen to me?

Kurt spoke first, and Gwen was impressed by his lengthy monologue on the uses of the computer as a tool for learning. He tried to allay any fears the more conservative men might have and to cut through their romantic loyalties to old-fashioned methods of teaching by giving repeated examples of how computers could be used creatively in all areas from mathematics to art. Phanor and the group were spellbound, and it wasn't until they approached the area of cost that Kurt began to waiver.

When Phanor prefaced his next barrage of questions by pointing out that Mexico, unlike the United States, was just on the edge of breaking out of Third World status and was struggling to build a strong economy, Gwen understood that he was talking money. Now he wanted to get down to figures and see if what he thought was a good idea could become a reality.

She knew that it was time for her presentation. She looked over at Kurt and, when he gave her an encouraging nod of approval, stood up and began. One by one, Gwen pulled out the charts that she had so carefully prepared and slowly, calmly, went over the comparison figures that she had spent so much time researching before the trip. Phanor's men lashed out with questions, and she answered accurately, intelligently, succinctly. Somehow she had located a calm place inside of her, and all of her anxiety and fear were gone. She was talking from a solid base of knowledge, and knew that there was no need to be insecure. Facts, after all, were facts. And while it couldn't be denied that there were ways of presenting costs to Tonkan's advantage, the key point was that over a long period of time the use of computers in the business itself, in the school system, and in other educational facilities was a sound financial investment and an imperative in keeping up with the times.

After what seemed to Gwen like hours, the questions tapered off, and she finally had a moment to catch her breath. When she looked over at Kurt, she saw to her shock that he was leaning back in his chair with his hands folded under his chin, coolly staring at her. On the other hand, Phanor's face shone with excitement as he again went over the graphs with another colleague.

"Muy bien," Phanor finally remarked, and looking down the table, he suggested that they stop for lunch. "I have arranged to have it sent in," he announced, and as thankful as Gwen was for the break, she wished that they could leave the room for a short change of scene. In the next few minutes, in what seemed like a flurry of activity, waiters appeared and quickly laid out the meal on the long table. The room was a buzz of Spanish as Phanor and his group discussed the merger. Gwen looked over at Kurt, and leaning toward him asked, "How do you think we're doing?"

"Looks all right to me," came his terse reply.

He turned his attention back to his plate and began devouring a spicy taco.

What on earth is wrong with him? Gwen thought, and made another attempt to speak to him. But her attention was diverted by the man sitting to her left, who had decided that it was his turn to air his misgivings about the merger.

Lunch was cleared as efficiently as it had been brought in, and soon they were back to business, going over some of the finer details of the operations. Although no one person took the floor in the afternoon, Gwen noticed that there was a subtle change in Phanor's focus of attention, and that with the exception of a few questions, he directed all of his conversation to her.

In the back of her mind the dynamics of the meeting disturbed her. She felt that something was seriously wrong. It was as if Kurt had faded into the background and now she was leading the negotiations for Tonkan. But there was nothing she could do. It was better to continue on as efficiently as possible than to try to defer to Kurt. It was her job to deal with Phanor with as much professionalism as was possible. She would try and figure out what exactly was going on with Kurt after the meeting.

After an arduous afternoon the meeting finally came to an end, and Gwen shook hands with the smiling Phanor and the rest of the men. They all lived in Guadalajara and were eager to get back to their families. Even Phanor seemed slightly anxious to get away, and Gwen was glad that they weren't expecting her to socialize with them at night, as she would have had to do with American businessmen.

"Well, Kurt," she said excitedly after she had noticed that they were the last to leave the room. "I think we impressed them. Don't you?"

"I'd say so," he said without looking at her.

What *is* the matter with him, she wondered frantically, and then went on, "Maybe we can even get an answer from them tomorrow."

"I'm sure that with your brand of determination it will be possible," Kurt declared, and turning his back to her, he left the room.

Gwen felt a pang of hurt course through her, and tried to hold back the build-up of hot tears that filled her eyes. She grasped at the edge of the table for support, knowing that she was on the verge of giving in to her emotions. But pride came to the rescue. Kurt had no right treating her like this, she decided. If he was bothered by something she'd said at the meeting, he should tell her so instead of behaving like a spoiled child. Instead of whimpering about her hurt feelings, she should be angry. Damn! She slammed her fist once on the table, turned on her heel, and stormed back to her room.

That afternoon Gwen tried to forget about what happened, but she couldn't, for a moment, put aside the annoying question of Kurt's behavior toward her during the somewhat lonely day. How could he turn on her after what they had shared? Or had he seen it only as a one-night stand, something to regret in the morning? No! He had been fine at breakfast—something had happened at the

meeting. A swim in the hotel pool preceded a nap
and then dinner in the hotel restaurant. She couldn't
help but compare her solitary meal to the exhil-
arating breakfast that morning, and all of her ef-
forts at cheerfulness soon turned to dismay.

It was not even ten o'clock when Gwen got
back to her room, and the minute she closed the
door she felt the restlessness coming on. The intensity of the day's activities had made her over-
tired, and she knew that she would have a hard
time getting to sleep. Although she had brought a
wonderful romance novel by her favorite author
to read, when she slipped into a warm lounging
robe, made herself comfortable on the bed, and
opened the book, she felt silly, almost ridiculous,
at having come all the way to Guadalajara only to
spend the night reading.

Instead, she began to think about Kurt and about
the day's activities. She went back in time to their
breakfast together and remembered the warm,
tender way he had treated her. Then came the
meeting, which, according to Gwen's memory,
had gone like clockwork, with Kurt first presenting his side of the argument and then throwing
the ball to her so that she could clinch the deal.
She tried to recall just when his attitude toward
her had changed. She scoured her memory for
any faux-pas she might be guilty of. Surely Kurt
wanted the deal to go through, she thought, and
should have been pleased by the success of her
presentation?

By the time Gwen was fully caught up in trying
to solve the mystery of Kurt's hostility, she was
up and pacing the room, driven by her need for

an explanation. When she looked at her watch, she saw that it was after eleven, and as always the voice of reason took over and reminded her that tomorrow would be another hard day and that she had better at least try and sleep.

But once in bed, she knew it was no use. She lay there, stiff and anxious, knowing that it would take a miracle for her to relax and fall asleep. The question of Kurt's behavior was just too important to the outcome of the project. If she and Kurt were going to work together, communications had to be cleared up. She would not put up with having to cater to his moods, not knowing what his response to her was going to be or if she was performing the way he wanted her to.

And of course, there was the small matter of her own longing for him . . .

In a moment of quick decision Gwen got up out of bed. The early spring night was chilly, and the cold tiles beneath her feet sent a tingling of goose bumps up her spine. She grabbed for a light wool sweater and a pair of jeans, stepped into leather thongs, and, pulling her fingers impatiently through her hair, walked across the room and out the door. She took no time to reconsider what she was about to do; instead she went directly through the suite and stood in front of Kurt's closed door.

At first Gwen tapped lightly, but when there was no answer she doubled up her hand into a fist and pounded angrily. Within seconds the door opened. Kurt stood in front of her, his face an expressionless mask. He quickly turned away, as if he wanted to avoid any direct eye contact.

"I have to talk with you," Gwen said quickly, afraid that he might close the door before she could tell him why she was there.

"Don't you think it's a little bit late?" he asked. Gwen had been right; the anger in his voice was unmistakable.

"Yes, I think it's late. But there's something we should get straightened out right away and it can't wait until morning. May I come in?"

"All right. Come in," he said, and stepped aside so she could enter the room. Kurt's bedroom was an exact duplicate of hers, though darker in tone and more somber in decor, so that the ceiling seemed lower and the walls pressed inward.

"Can I get you something?" Kurt asked politely, waving his arm in the direction of the bar.

"No. No, thank you." Gwen perched herself on the edge of the chair that partnered a beautiful antique rolltop desk. "I don't know exactly how to begin," she said, "but something is bothering you and I want to know what it is. I did my best at the meeting today so that we would get the contract, and I think Phanor is going to sign. But somewhere along the line I must have done or said something that disturbed you. I really don't want to have to put up with your cold-shoulder routine all day tomorrow, so if you'll tell me what it is, maybe we can work through it." Gwen's words were calm and businesslike, but inside she was screaming. Kurt, please, talk to me. I can't bear your coldness, she thought, but her pride would not let her plead.

All the time she was speaking, Kurt kept his back to her. It was impossible for him to keep from hearing what she had to say, but he gave her no indication that he felt pressed in any way to respond. He walked over to the bar, and after dropping two ice cubes into a tall glass, he covered them with scotch and then an inch of water.

Gwen stood waiting for his reply, and as she waited her anger began to flare. He had hurt her, and now he wouldn't even give her the courtesy of an explanation.

When Kurt turned back after mixing his drink, the expression on his face had changed. Instead of the cold, steely mask he had worn when Gwen walked in, he was sporting a slight half smile that confused Gwen even more. Kurt took a large swallow of his drink and said, "I thought you were quite the success today, Gwen. Congratulations. I didn't know that you could be so forceful or so effective." Was she imagining the sarcastic edge she thought she heard in his voice? Rather than acknowledge his compliment, she waited patiently for him to go on.

Finally, he did. "Oh, I don't know why I was short with you, Gwen. I guess I just got tired at some point or another. Really, I have nothing against you personally. It was Phanor and his gang who started to get on my nerves."

Gwen looked up into his eyes, and instinct told her that he was lying. "You're not being honest with me," she said bravely, but she couldn't keep her voice from shaking.

Kurt appeared to be wrestling with a decision during the long silence that followed. Finally he spoke. "I have something I want to tell you, Gwen. It won't take long, but I think it will explain my behavior." He took Gwen's arm, led her to a chair, and pulled up another alongside her.

"About three years ago, when I had just reached the position of associate vice-president at Tonkan, another woman came to work for the firm in your old job as administrative assistant. She was, like you, intelligent, ambitious, and beautiful. But Angie had one more quality that you don't have. She was totally ruthless.

"Angie came from a small town in Texas, and her father, who had once been wealthy, somehow lost all of his money. Oh, they weren't hungry or anything—that might actually have been better. They just weren't able to maintain anything approaching their former way of life. Angie was old enough to remember the good times, and young enough to believe that money would give her everything she wanted. She figured that the more money you have, the more friends you have, the more time you have, and the more power you have.

"When her dad went under, Angie began to hate him, and apparently she decided then that she was going to have to make it on her own. According to her, women were not only clearly the stronger sex, but men were too damn weak to have anything to do with except as vehicles for getting ahead.

"That was Angie's philosophy when she arrived at Tonkan."

Gwen saw Kurt wince, sensed how his muscles tightened as he continued, and she braced herself for what she knew was not going to be a happy ending to his story.

"I guess I should tell you too, in all honesty, that Angie was a real beauty—and a pretty good actress, too. When she walked through the office, every eye was on her—and every man wanted her. I could tell you, Gwen, that I was young, and I could go on until I'm blue in the face finding excuses for my part in this little drama. But to make a long story short, I fell for her—hard. When she seemed interested in me, I really thought we could build a relationship. At one point, I even thought we were in love.

"Well, I batted zero on that one." There was an edge of bitterness in his voice now, and at the same time he looked slightly ashamed. "We went together for about six months, and we were beginning to be known around Tonkan as a couple. Oddly enough, no one seemed to care, so we weren't worried about breaking policy. About that time Angie started complaining about her job, saying that it was getting boring and that she was ready to move up. Granted, she was smart, and had been doing good work, but she wasn't ready for the jump to associate vice-president, and I knew it then.

"But somehow she convinced me to try and help her make the move, and I did. I made it possible for her to be promoted by swinging a deal and giving her credit for it."

"Oh, Kurt," Gwen said softly. The look on his face was so tortured now that she longed to take him in her arms and comfort him. But she was not sure enough to make the first move and could only hope that somehow simply telling the story would help him.

"After the promotion, things between us changed suddenly. It was as if she wasn't interested in me anymore. She had gotten what she wanted, and was ready to move on up to the next guy, and milk *him* for the next promotion. Well, you get the picture, don't you? Just about that time I began to wise up, and when I did, I swore that that kind of thing would never happen to me again."

"And Angie? What happened to her?" Gwen was almost afraid to ask.

"Nothing good. Angie got a little reckless in her game playing. She coaxed the president of the company into bed, his wife found out about it, and all I heard after that was that she was fired from Tonkan and blackballed from the industry. Funny," Kurt added, "as I think about it now, I actually feel sorry for Angie."

"Well . . ." Gwen sighed deeply. "That certainly does explain a lot. But Kurt, I still can't believe that you actually thought that I was another Angie, or that I was out to use you. You know how hard I work, and"—now her voice trembled—"I would never, never do a thing like that."

"Oh, Gwen. I knew that what I had to say might hurt you." He reached out for her hand and brought it to his lips. "Try and realize that what happened today was a mistake, a reflex instilled by a bad experience. It had nothing to do with you."

"I think I understand." Gwen made no effort to remove the hand that he was still holding, nor did she resist when Kurt stood up and pulled her to her feet. She wanted to believe him, believe that the pain in his voice had been real, and strong enough to excuse his behavior. But most of all, she wanted him.

"Thank you for understanding," he whispered against her ear, and bent down to seal their new accord with a kiss.

Gwen's responsive mouth rose to meet his lips, and their reunion was complete. Kurt moved his lips slowly, expertly, over hers, and she opened to him, allowing his tongue to journey inside her mouth and sample her very essence. Then one hand was cradling the back of her head, fingers playing gently with her hair, while the other arm fell to her waist, caught her in a semicircular trap, and held her close so that she could feel the rhythmic thumping from within his chest. And, strangely, it seemed that her own heartbeat fell into synchrony.

"Kurt?" she whispered, wondering if he felt what she did, and his hand cradled her breast, circling till her nipple rose to his fingers' touch. She shuddered as he covered her mouth with his own and pulled her deep within the current of his dark, swirling passion.

Then, though she could not say how, they were standing in front of Kurt's bed. Kurt broke their embrace one last time for a long search into her eyes, and his earlier fierce expression changed to one of tender concern. "You do want this?" he asked, and Gwen threw her arms around his neck in gratitude.

She knew that she would not have been able to resist if he had come to her without apology or explanation, even after what had happened. But the fact that he had asked, had understood that his respect for her was as important to her as his desire for her, freed her totally. The knowledge that she would have no regrets, that she could take her joy with no loss of pride, freed her to give in to the desire that was mounting inside her.

"Yes, I want you," she said in a soft, clear voice, and with no further hesitation Kurt raised her sweater up over her head, and then quickly shed his own clothing while she finished undressing. When they were naked, they stood quiescent, staring at one another.

"You're so lovely," Kurt said as he lowered his lips to her breasts and just barely touched an erect nipple with the tip of his tongue. And with that faintest of touches it was as if they had joined hands and stepped off the edge of the planet, out into a star-studded universe where meteors swirled, lights flashed, and the sun gave off a brilliant yellow heat that tattooed their bodies with molten kisses.

Gwen's deep moan of pleasure filled the room as Kurt lowered her onto the bed. Her hungry hands raked over his body, and he growled back in response, capturing them in one hand and pinning them over her head. Then, as he looked deeply into her eyes, he roamed over her body with his other hand, seeking the hidden places that sent her twisting into an oblivion of pleasure. He showered her lips, her eyelids, her neck with tiny kisses and whispered hoarsely, "Gwen, show me that you want me . . . Darling, make love to me . . ." and he lowered himself into her, releasing her hands to crush her to him.

"Oh, yes," she moaned, and reared up to meet him. When they came together, the planets in Gwen's dark universe collided and shattered into millions of splinters of light that coursed through her entire body and left her feeling wildly, ecstatically alive. The rivulets of light carried a heat that seeped into her muscles and melted her down so that she could open herself up to Kurt, so deep and so wide that she became frightened and a tiny whimper escaped her.

"There, there," he whispered to her, soothing her with mouth and hands until once more she knew only the deep release of her passion and the unbearable pleasure of his lovemaking. What had started as a tumultuous blast into the heavens was transformed into a soft, gentle fall into paradise. The quiet pianissimo of their final chord echoed throughout the room, and together they lay swaying in one another's arms, as if they were destined to stay there forever.

It seemed to Gwen as if time stood still during the next few moments, as if it were light-years later that she heard Kurt ask, "Okay?"

She squirmed under him to straighten out an arm. "Wonderful," she crooned, and planted a quick kiss on his smooth shoulder.

"Gwen," Kurt said, pulling himself up a little. "Promise me that you'll let me show you the town tomorrow night. Beautiful Guadalajara . . . we'll paint it red."

"I promise," Gwen said sleepily, and tried to stifle a yawn.

"Oh, darling, you're so tired." Kurt reached over and rearranged the pillow under her head. "Shhh," he soothed her, and then began to stroke her hair. "We've got to rest now," he whispered, and within moments they were both fast asleep.

Chapter Four

❦

Gwen woke up early the next morning and found it hard to believe that she was in Kurt's bed. She had fallen into a deep, dreamless sleep the night before that left her feeling refreshed and relaxed, and she lay on her back blinking back at the new day, smiling peacefully to herself. Kurt and she had rolled apart during the night and now he was lying on his stomach with one arm flung over his head, so that Gwen couldn't see his face. Her first impulse was to reach out and touch him, to run her hand down the long slope of his spine. But when she glanced over at the clock and saw that it was only six, she resisted the temptation. They had a long day ahead of them: she should let him sleep.

She lay awake for some time, hoping that she would fall back to sleep. But the memory of the night before set her pulse racing. She felt like a neglected, dying plant that had been revived by a warm, life-giving rain. When she finally decided that she was awake for the day, she got up quietly and picked up her clothing from the floor. She dressed quickly, being careful not to make noise so that she wouldn't wake Kurt.

When she got back to her own room, she shrugged on her terry-cloth bathrobe and sat down with a batch of papers from her briefcase. She was glad she had a little time to herself. More than anything, she wanted to settle the deal today; that way they might even have a day left over for leisure. But as she went over her reports once more, wanting to be certain of her figures, she found it difficult to concentrate. She couldn't believe that everything was working out so smoothly.

When she finished reading the last page, she let the papers fall to her lap and, for a moment, put her head back. It was Kurt who really needed some thinking about, but any logical notions about the right or wrong of what had happened the night before quickly dissipated into a sensual memory of the pleasure she had experienced. Gwen still felt a tinge of anxiety when she reminded herself of all of the problems that any kind of an affair with Kurt could create for her at work. Still, she knew that she was not capable of stopping after their brief encounter, and that if last night was a sample of what lay ahead for them, she wanted more of it. After all, they would be discreet, and wasn't the important thing the way they felt about each other? And hadn't they worked out the most important problem already?

Lost in her daydreams, Gwen didn't notice that time was passing, and when she looked again at the clock, she jumped up in alarm. What was she thinking, lolling about for so long? Now she would really have to move if she wanted to make breakfast.

She rushed through her shower, and several

minutes later was stepping into low-heeled, dark green pumps as she pulled a simple matching sheath dress over her head. As she grabbed for her things and rushed out of her room past Kurt's door, she wondered if she should have woken him when she left, after all. Stop worrying! she told herself.

When she approached the dining room she saw that Kurt was already eating, and that he had been joined at the large table by Phanor and Arzelia. Gwen walked over to the table feeling a bit self-conscious when she saw that all eyes were on her.

"Good morning," she said, and quickly sat down. She was greeted by a chorus of good mornings, with the most enthusiastic welcome coming from Phanor.

"Hello," he said warmly, and gave her a little bow. "We've just been talking about you."

"Raving about you is more like it," Kurt piped in, and smiled his hello with a special warmth she knew was only for her eyes.

"My dear"—Phanor radiated an ebullient mood—"I can't tell you how impressed I was by your presentation yesterday. Not only did you answer all of our questions, you managed to convince everyone that we have no choice in the matter. Only a fool would reject your offer."

Gwen heaved a sigh of relief. The deal was going to go through, and she had made a good impression. But as Phanor continued to sing her praises far beyond what she thought was necessary, she became acutely uncomfortable.

"I must tell you," he was saying, "that I haven't

had much opportunity to deal with female representatives. You know our social structure here in
Mexico is, shall we say, somewhat more rigid than
yours. But if you are an example of the newly
'liberated' woman, I am all for it. Once again
I commend you on your performance, and I want
to say that when we get down to the particu-
lars of this merger, I want to work very closely
with you and will even recommend that you come
back after we start operations." He flashed Gwen
another brilliant smile, and then looked over at
Kurt as if asking for support of his opinion.

"Oh yes," Kurt said, "we all think Gwen is a
terrific girl and a hard worker. We're very pleased
with the way she's been coming along."

Gwen brought her cup down hard on its saucer
when she heard Kurt's words. Her face flushed
hot with rage. Had he really referred to her as a
girl? And what exactly did he mean by "she's
coming along," she fumed. But there was nothing
she could say or do. This was certainly not the
time or place to start an argument. She turned her
attention back to her now-unwanted breakfast and
tried to calm herself. After all, it was just a question of semantics, and she was sure she could
explain to Kurt privately that his choice of words
had been poor, to say the least.

Just then, at the close of a humorous anecdote,
Kurt threw Gwen a quick, seductive wink that no
one at the table could have missed. After everything they had said about the necessity for discretion! He was deliberately making her look like a
talented secretary who was using her boss to get
ahead. Anger propelled her up and out of her

chair. "I'd like to freshen up before we begin," she said, and headed toward the ladies' room. How could he? she wondered as she sat on the edge of a settee and took several deep breaths in an effort to calm down. Was he really so insensitive that he didn't realize how he was treating her? Hadn't their discussion taught him anything? She knew she had to steel herself for the day ahead, no matter how deeply wounded she felt, no matter how little she felt like working. Today's meetings were crucial and she had to ignore everything except the business at hand. She would deal with Kurt later.

The meeting went much the same as the one the day before. Phanor seemed to address most of his remarks to Gwen, and she was embarrassed when she realized that she had become Tonkan's spokesman, almost as if Kurt wasn't there. She tried to put her best foot forward, but she felt unsettled and edgy under the scrutiny of Kurt's critical stare.

Lunch was again brought in, but Gwen found that she had little appetite. She glanced over at Kurt, to see him involved in conversation with Arzelia and was relieved when the meeting started again. By now it had been decided that Phanor and everyone at Productos Mexicanos was interested in collaborating with Tonkan. What lay ahead was a long road of splinter negotiations to determine the extent of the involvement; whether they would begin by using Tonkan equipment or take a gamble and set up plans for their own factory. They also had to discuss what kind of profit percentages could be worked out, and if Phanor wanted a full-time representative from Tonkan to act as a consultant and move to Guadalajara. Gwen's head began to spin at the sweeping scale of the job ahead, and she felt slightly overwhelmed by it all.

But as head of his company, Phanor took everything in his stride, and Gwen sat back in quiet admiration as he spelled out the stages of future operations with calm assurance. Finally, in the early afternoon, he told them that he would now like to break up the meeting for the day so that they could take a little time off. He thanked the Tonkan representatives warmly, saying that he realized that their jobs dealt mainly with public relations and that they were, as he put it, "the ground-breakers." He hoped that they could meet again the next day at his home and lay out a preliminary outline for their procedure.

Gwen shook Phanor's hand as she left the room and gave him a warm smile. She was really beginning to like him and looked forward to seeing his home the following day. "You and I will talk more tomorrow," he said to her after taking her aside from the group, and she knew immediately what he had in mind. Lord! she thought. Who would have imagined that on my first assignment I would manage to impress someone enough to make him want to talk to me about a job. She knew that in large corporate dealings it didn't matter whether the firms were allies or enemies; when an exceptional employee came along, they would bribe, beg, or steal to get him. And Gwen was just beginning to realize that she fell into that category.

She noticed that Kurt had disappeared, and

sighed. It was probably for the best. He had already succeeded in dampening the lighthearted enthusiasm she had felt that morning, and she still couldn't figure out why he was doing it. It couldn't be professional jealousy—they had disposed of that last night. Her only option was to at least try and enjoy the rest of the afternoon.

When she walked toward the pool area a few minutes later, heads turned, and she knew that she had chosen the right bathing suit. It had taken her a long time to decide on the two-piece, but when she had seen herself in the mirror in the bright floral suit that set off her figure to perfection, she'd simply had to buy it.

For the rest of the afternoon she tried to forget everything: Tonkan, Phanor, and most of all, Kurt. She swam laps for a while, losing herself in the monotonous but soothing physical motion, then, tired from the night before, fell asleep as she lay under the sun. She awoke, saw that luckily she had acquired a healthy glow but had not burned, and headed back to her room.

She spent another hour browsing in the gift shop. "We'll paint the town red," echoed in her memory, and she recalled her promise to Kurt from the night before. She wouldn't break the date, she finally decided. A night on the town was just too tempting. Instead, she would try temporarily to forget about their differences, and give him a chance to explain later. When she looked at her watch and discovered that she had only half an hour before dinner, she set off for her room at once to change.

She got ready in record time and started to cut

through their suite, but saw that Kurt's door was closed. I'll go down to the lobby to wait, she thought, and walked toward the elevator. In the fluorescent lights of the hallway her red dress turned a bright scarlet, and made her feel slightly gaudy, and a little risqué. But once downstairs, standing in the soft glow of the half-lit courtyard, the dress's brightness faded into a deep, rich red. Gwen touched the skirt of her beautiful gown and knew that she had never worn anything lovelier. Sparks of interest in the eyes of the men who strolled by assured her that she wore it well, and made her feel attractive, even beautiful.

"You look enchanting," Kurt said as he approached her. He offered her a little bow and clicked his heels like castanets to punctuate his compliment.

"You look pretty nice yourself." Gwen took his arm. It was apparent that he was going to say nothing about the events of the day. He wore a crisp cotton shirt, unbuttoned at the neck, along with tan, tapered slacks, and carried a matching jacket over his arm. The simple lines of the stark white shirt emphasized the clean, clear cut of his profile and the ebony denseness of his dark eyes. As always, her attraction to him was instant and electric.

"This way, madame." Kurt bowed low and led Gwen to the restaurant. "If this place weren't so good, I would have been tempted to eat out. But I don't think we'd do better anywhere in Guadalajara."

"It's got my vote," Gwen agreed as they stepped into the dining room and saw that tonight it was decorated in a tribute to one of Mexico's most famous pastimes, the bullfight. Gwen's eyes grew wide with interest as the waiter led them across the room and sat them at a quiet, intimate corner table.

"Oh, Kurt, look!" Gwen exclaimed as she pointed to the ruby-red cape that hung on the wall facing them.

"Um-hmm," Kurt said, and looked across the table at her as if he was amused by her excitement. "Those long, tapered poles over there"—he pointed to another wall—"are the instruments of the picador." Gwen strained her neck to catch a glimpse.

"You know," she said, "I feel as if I can almost hear the roaring of the crowds in the background."

When, a bare moment later, a smiling waiter appeared, Kurt ordered two margaritas. "I hope that's okay," he said when he realized that he hadn't consulted Gwen.

"Oh, yes. I'm beginning to get used to the Mexican taste in food and drink. It certainly has character," she added, and then laughed out loud. "What I mean is, the food is hot and the drink is strong."

Kurt laughed. "Gwen," he said after a moment, and reached out and covered her hand with his. "I didn't know that you were so interested in the bullfights. It was the last thing I thought that a woman as, well, modern, as you, might want to see. Otherwise I would have arranged for tickets. But as it is now, our schedule is so tight I don't know if it's even possible."

"Oh, it's all right, Kurt. When I really think

about it, I probably would hate all that violence."
She took a little sip of her drink. "I guess my
curiosity is just a throwback from books I've read
about it—particularly Hemingway. He made it all
sound so exciting, and so . . . romantic."

"He did," Kurt agreed, and buttered the corner
of a piece of bread. "That's why I went to them
when I first started coming here. But I've never
found anything romantic about them. As a matter
of fact, the heat, the crowds, the noise—and particularly the cruelty to the bulls—finally drove me
away."

Kurt's honesty and his unwillingness to accept
the macho mystique of the cruel sport impressed
Gwen. "Perhaps," she said hesitantly, "it's something better read about than seen. Or perhaps it
simply doesn't belong in this day and age."

Kurt touched his glass to hers and said, "Olé."
Gwen echoed him, then giggled, breaking the somber mood they had fallen into, as she realized that
half the restaurant had heard them.

Just then they heard what sounded like a little
cough, and looked up to see the waiter standing
alongside their table, ready to take their order.

"I kept thinking we were forgetting something,"
said Kurt, and handed Gwen one of the menus.
"We'll be ready in a few moments," he assured
the waiter, and they turned their attention to the
menus and tried to look deadly serious about making up their minds quickly.

"I think I'll just have the steak, and a little
salad. I know they tell you not to eat raw vegetables, but I don't think it will be a problem here."
Gwen finally said.

"My, but we are conservative tonight, aren't we?" Kurt teased her. "I'm going to be adventuresome and try the turkey casserole *molé*," he said almost proudly.

"What's that?" Gwen asked.

"Well, as you probably already know, turkey is native to Mexico, as is their famous *molé*, the chocolate sauce that's served with it."

Gwen couldn't refrain from making a face.

"I know," said Kurt. "Most Americans can't even bear to look at it. But you'll see. I'll let you taste mine."

"No, no thank you," Gwen said. "I think I'll stick to my steak and save the chocolate for dessert."

As it turned out, the meal was prepared quickly and was served with the characteristic elegance of the restaurant. At one point a young guitarist slipped into the room and began playing softly. Although she could not understand the words, Gwen was certain they were love songs.

"How beautiful!" she said when her plate was put before her. In the center of the platter was the beefsteak she had ordered, served in the Mexican way, with lemon wedges. It was garnished with bright green and red vegetables, including fresh sprigs of parsley and tiny bright orange peppers. "Whoever said color was a stimulus to the appetite was right," she said as she lunged into her meal, feeling suddenly famished.

"Oh, yes," Kurt murmured after taking a careful, deliberate sampling of his strange-looking dish. Gwen had never seen gravy look so rich and dark, or so . . . chocolaty. "This is the real thing." Taking a bite, he made a sound of pleasure, and then said, "Are you sure you don't want a taste, Gwen?"

"Maybe later," she pleaded, hoping he wouldn't press her. Although she was usually adventuresome when it came to food, *molé* was one dish that she had definitely decided to pass on.

For a long time they ate silently, and Gwen thought to herself how nice it was that neither seemed to feel pressed to make conversation when it wasn't necessary. From time to time she caught the subtle scent of the roses that grew in a nearby garden, noticed the heavy weight and satin feel of the old silver flatware, rested her eyes on the colors and textures of the beautiful room. She felt as if she had walked into a romantic fantasy in which all of the senses were pampered and catered to.

But then the vision would be shattered by the thought that she had yet to resolve the matter of Kurt's patronizing behavior to her earlier in the day. She knew that she mustn't let too much time go by before they talked about it.

"Everything okay?" Kurt broke into her thoughts, and she smiled over at him. "Wonderful," she said softly. Gwen allowed herself a brief moment to experience the full impact of his strong, charismatic presence, and in that moment realized that she had already given herself up to a night of love.

"I'm glad you like it," Kurt said, and finishing up the last bite of his meal, quickly glanced down at his watch. "Looks like we're going to have to get going, though, or we'll wind up missing everything."

The mere thought of missing a moment of their night on the town made Gwen impatient. At her urging, they even decided to wait until later to have their coffee, and after a quick touch-up of her makeup, she was more than ready to go.

"Are you prepared for a big night?" Kurt asked as he hailed a cab.

"I think so," Gwen said, her eyes shining.

"Off we go then." He helped her into the cab, his hand resting briefly at the base of her spine, starting tingles coursing through her every nerve. He spoke momentarily to the driver in Spanish, and then sat back in the seat beside her.

"His name is José. He's going to give us a little tour of the city before he lets us off. I wanted you to see it."

Gwen smiled her thanks and turned her attention to the splendor of the old, colonial city that lay peacefully nestled in the Valley of Jalisco. All of the houses were built around central patios, and their well-kept gardens seemed to cover every spare inch of ground.

"Look, Kurt!" Gwen almost shouted as they passed a particularly magnificent house with a garden that was bursting with color.

"Roses, gardenias, poinciana . . ." Gwen began to identify the flowers.

"And look there, quick." Kurt pointed out the window. "Have you ever seen a raintree before?"

"No," she replied, and then, "How beautiful!" The tree was covered with blossoms of gold that took her breath away.

Now they were traveling through the outer circle of side streets that bordered the central, downtown section of the city. "These are all typical houses," Kurt said, and told the driver to stop in front of one that was surrounded by a high stone wall.

"This is the house and the museum of the famous Mexican muralist, Orozco," Kurt said, and Gwen nodded. "He was one of Mexico's greatest artists, and has a huge fresco in the Governor's Palace that we'll see when we get downtown."

Gwen gave Kurt an "I'm impressed" smile, and he responded warmly. "I never knew you were so cultured," she said after they started driving again.

"Oh yes," he replied. "I have very fine taste . . . in everything." He reached over and took her hand in his.

Will he kiss me? Gwen wondered, but their moment ended abruptly with the blare of honking horns and squealing brakes. They were approaching *el centro.*

"Now we're coming to the Plaza de Armes where the bands play and the mariachis gather." Kurt reverted back to his role as tour guide. "And there is a statue of Father Hidalgo."

"Who?" Gwen asked, thinking that her Mexican history was certainly rusty.

"You might say that he was the Mexican version of our Lincoln," he answered. "He did a lot to end slavery here and improve the lives of the very poor."

"Did you just memorize a guidebook or something?" Gwen said teasingly, once again impressed by Kurt's seemingly vast storehouse of knowledge about Mexico. Kurt just laughed.

"Driver," he called out as they turned a corner

and entered a street that was aglare with bright lights. "We'll stop here," he said, and reached in his pocket for his wallet. The broad smile of thanks on José's face suggested that Kurt had been generous with him, and Gwen waved her own friendly good-bye to the round-faced man.

Kurt clasped Gwen's hand in his own large one, and said, "Try and stay close to me." The streets were teeming with tourists, peddlers, shoppers, beggars, troubadours, and a variety of other strollers out to enjoy the nightlife of the magic city.

Gwen soon began to absorb the electric energy that permeated the atmosphere. Her eyes grew wide with excitement, and she clutched at Kurt's arm both in an effort to stay with him and also to try and contain her desire to run and twirl and leap, like the heroine in a madcap musical.

"Aren't they beautiful," Gwen said to Kurt and pointed to the wool shawls that were laid out for display on an old blanket. Sitting on her haunches, crouched over them, was a young Indian woman who looked up at them through doelike eyes.

"*Habla Espanol?*" Kurt bent down and spoke to the woman.

"*Sí,*" she responded, and the rest of their exchange was lost to Gwen. Kurt rattled on in perfect Spanish, and the seemingly shy woman began to respond with a torrent of words that went on forever, as if she had finally gotten her chance to speak and meant to make the most of it. Kurt nodded his head sympathetically, indicating his understanding. Finally the woman seemed to be winding down, and she fell back into silence as abruptly as she had started talking.

"She's from the state of Chiapas, way down by the Guatamalan border, and she's from the Tenehapan tribe. Her name's Antonia," Kurt said to Gwen. Putting a hand on Gwen's shoulder, he looked down at the woman and said, "Gwen."

"Gwen," the woman tried to say her name, and Gwen smiled at the strange-sounding pronunciation.

"She tells me that she's a backstrap weaver," Kurt said. "She and her friends take their looms and tie up to trees on the side of mountains and sit there working for what probably amounts to a good portion of their lives. . . ." He seemed dazed by the utter simplicity of such an existence.

"Look at this one." Gwen spotted a white shawl that lay half hidden under the rest. When she pulled it out, she was amazed by the complicated pattern of design that was woven into the material.

"They all mean something," Kurt said as he passed his fingers over the brightly colored hieroglyphs that waltzed across the white background. He bent down again and said something to Antonia, and then reached into his wallet and handed her several Mexican bills.

"Gwen," Kurt said, "I want you to have it. It's a present from me; a memento of your trip here."

"Oh, Kurt, I couldn't . . ." Gwen started, but he raised a hand to hush her.

"It's already done," he insisted, and after saying good-bye to Antonia, he grabbed Gwen's arm and said, "Come on. We've got lots more to see tonight."

Gwen and Kurt spent the next hour wandering around the streets, stopping to pick up occasional trinkets or to listen to a particularly good band. It *was* like a series of shows at a circus, Gwen thought as she swallowed the last of her *café con leche*. Feeling slightly hungry from their walk, Kurt had suggested that they stop for a *torta*, and Gwen had instantly agreed. She found the little sandwich delectable, and ate it all, though an hour ago she would have sworn she'd never be able to eat another bite.

"Over there's the market," Kurt said, pointing across the street at what looked like a swarming beehive of activity that extended for blocks. "We'll try and go there sometime during the day." They were walking down a side street that wasn't quite so crowded. Suddenly Gwen's heel slipped and she pitched forward. Kurt reacted quickly, reaching out in time to keep her from falling.

"I have a faint recollection of doing this before," he joked after seeing that she wasn't hurt. Gwen, too, remembered her near spill on the airplane; the first accidental fall into his arms. Only, unlike the first time, Kurt did not release her; instead he wrapped her more snugly in his arms and there, standing under the dimly lit streetlight, he lowered his head and parted his lips to cover her trembling mouth. His touch was warm, and he tasted like the sweet coffee that they had been sipping moments before.

Gwen reached up and put a hand on his shoulder in order to keep her balance. All he has to do is come near me, she thought, and I weaken. She turned her head to deepen the kiss. After a moment Kurt pulled his face away and, taking a little nip at the end of her nose, said, "You know what I'm going to show you now?"

He looked so pleased in his role of host that Gwen widened her eyes and answered with exaggerated enthusiasm, "What?"

"Come right this way." He took her arm again and led her toward their next destination. "I'm about to give you a real taste of Mexican nightlife."

The club that they started with was small, and was called *La Estrella*. "The star," Gwen translated, and took her place on the stool alongside Kurt. The chairs stood in front of a long bar that ran the length of the room on either side of a stage and dance floor. Gwen saw that there were several other couples there who looked like they might be Americans, and they all nodded their hellos, as if glad to find kindred spirits in such a strange new land.

The man who came on stage holding his guitar was dressed in the black and red costume of a flamenco dancer. His tight pants hugged his muscular legs, and the short bolero jacket accented the breadth of his shoulders. But he was not there to dance; he was going to sing. And he did, Gwen thought, like no one she had ever heard before. The clear tenor of his voice rang through the room, as fresh and melodic as the chirping of an early-morning songbird, announcing the arrival of the sun. But even more usual, Gwen thought, was the deep feeling behind the voice. She was moved to tears when he sang the sad tale of two lovers who were separated by war and became bewildered when, in time, their memories of one another began to fade away. When the singer broke

into the strains of *"Morenita Mía"* and Kurt leaned
over to translate, "My dark-haired woman, I will
never forget you," Gwen fell madly, passionately,
in love with Mexico.

It took some urging on Kurt's part to get her to
leave the club, but he assured her that there was
more elsewhere, so she relented and followed him
out to the street and on to the next stop on
the strip. It didn't take her long to get caught up
in the fun of poking her head in every club to take
a look at the entertainment that was being offered.
In the last place they were in, they had actually
joined a band of mariachis in the final chorus of
the beautiful ode to the city, "Guadalajara," receiv-
ing good-natured boos from the audience.

Gwen's beautiful red dress was attracting attention, and several times during the evening she
caught Kurt looking at her with half-closed eyes,
as if he were planning its slow removal, or even
imagining her without it.

"Come on, Gwen, just one more stop," Kurt
insisted four clubs and two margaritas later. Gwen
was beginning to feel a bit tired, but despite her
fatigue, she was thrilled by the huge nightclub
constructed to look like a Greek ampitheater, with
high walls that were painted with colorful murals
depicting Mexico's dramatic history. Gwen found
herself applauding vigorously during the variety
show, which included everything from dancers to
magicians, and even Mexican comedians whom
she could barely understand. Afterward she and
Kurt danced, and several men cut in on him with
no reserve. Kurt began to do the same, and they

didn't find one another until several songs later, when she was already dead on her feet.

By the time they hailed a cab to return to the hotel, Gwen was floating somewhere between exhilaration and complete exhaustion.

"Thank you for a wonderful time, señorita." Kurt smiled and, putting his arm around her shoulders, pulled her to him. She looked up into his face and accepted his long, gentle kiss. "I've got to get you to bed," he whispered, and pulled her even closer. The cab stopped in front of the hotel, and Gwen got out and fell into silent step alongside Kurt as they walked through the lobby and took the elevator to their suite.

"You'll stay with me?" He turned to her and reached up to tuck in a strand of delinquent hair.

"Yes," Gwen said in response to the invitation of his strong arms, his soft, cool mouth. "But tomorrow we're going to have to talk," she added, remembering the important, unfinished business between them.

"Yes. I agree. We're going to have to talk," Kurt said, and swept her into his arms, "tomorrow. . . ."

Chapter Five

❦

"I'm so glad you could come," Señora Phanor
said to Gwen as they strolled through the garden
that was an extension of the courtyard of the
Phanor home. Beatriz spoke English, and Gwen
was glad for the company of the beautiful Mexican woman. Although Beatriz epitomized the gra-
ciousness of old-world Spanish culture, she also
shared some of the informality of modern times,
and Gwen found it easy to talk to her.

The house reflected much the same mix. Although Phanor's home was a classic of Spanish
architecture, the family collected contemporary
Mexican art, and the walls of the *sala* were lined
with beautiful abstract paintings.

Beatriz had taken an immediate liking to Gwen,
chattering animatedly in a way that Gwen found
irresistible. This visit to the Phanor home was the
second time she had left the hotel, and she had
been intrigued and excited by the tour they had
taken through the streets of Guadalajara on their
way there.

After a while Arzelia joined Gwen and her
mother in the garden, and the two women quizzed
Gwen about her life and work, curious to learn

more about what it was like to be a woman working in the world of business. In speaking with Beatriz, who had raised three other children besides Arzelia, Gwen thought about the vast differences between them and compared Beatriz's arranged marriage and total dedication to her husband and family to her own yearning for independence.

"Come inside now," Beatriz interrupted their chat. "Lunch will be ready soon."

The women joined Kurt and Phanor, who were returning from a tour of the stables. As they approached, Phanor was still in the middle of a monologue about bullfighting, but when he saw Gwen he stopped talking.

"You come with me," he said, and draped his arm through hers. "I want to make sure we get seated next to one another at lunch." As they walked slowly to the house Gwen took a quick glimpse at Kurt, and saw him frown.

She knew that it had to be Phanor's attention to her that was still bothering him. It seemed that no amount of lovemaking could cover up the competition he still brought to their relationship; they were going to have to talk the problem through as soon as possible. She turned to Phanor with a smile and allowed him to guide her into the spacious dining room.

Large platters of beef and chicken enchiladas, tostadas, *arroz con pollo*, and refried beans sat steaming on the table, and Gwen's mouth began to water as soon as she smelled the food. Phanor did indeed seat Gwen next to him, and after the oth-

ers were settled and a word of thanks had been
given by Beatriz, everyone dug in.

At the table, Gwen noticed that Kurt seemed to
be less outgoing than usual. Sitting across from
him, she was able to gauge his change in mood.
Was she imagining that he seemed to be avoiding
her glance, she wondered, and then decided to
turn her attention to her food. She concentrated
on the delicious meal, finishing just as Beatriz
suggested that they take their *café con leche* out
onto the patio.

The group went out together to the little patio
adjacent to the courtyard and sat in a circle that
overlooked the garden. Phanor again claimed possession of Gwen's attention and insisted that they
pull their chairs a little aside so that they could
talk.

"I gather that you know by now how impressed
I've been with your work," he began, and Gwen
knew immediately where the conversation was
going. "Yes," she responded warmly, "and I'd
like to thank you for all of the encouragement and
goodwill. All of us at Tonkan are looking forward
to working with you."

"Well," Phanor said as he took a sip of the rich,
brown brew, "we're looking forward to it, too.
But to be more specific, I would like to work with
you again, and have suggested in the report I'm
sending back that you be selected to head the
group who will return in six months and get down
to the brass tacks of this deal."

He paused for a moment and then went on.
"What I'd really like to do, though, is to convince
you to join us permanently at Productos Mexicanos,

either as the representative of Tonkan or, preferably, as an employee of our company." He pulled his chair a little closer to hers and then said, "You've no idea, Gwen what an asset you'd be to our company at this stage of the game. We've had a lot of public pressure on us lately to put a woman in a top executive position, and the timing is perfect, what with our switch-over to computers and plans to restructure the hierarchy of our operation."

Gwen studied his face for a moment and then said noncommittally, "your offer is very flattering." She tried to disguise the questions lurking behind her response. Why was he doing all this for her? After all, they hardly knew one another.

"I suppose you wonder why I'm making you such an offer." Phanor seemed to have read her mind. As he spoke, he traced a pattern on the ground with the toe of his shoe, realizing that he too was uneasy. "I'm afraid the answer is rather personal. I love my daughters. But to be honest with you, Gwen, I had so much hope for both of them—especially for Arzelia. She's got a mind as quick as a whip, and at first she seemed interested in working with me at the company. I, of course, would have given her free rein, and she could have moved fast, just like you have. But after a couple of years of it I guess she got tired, and now, as you see, she only puts in a perfunctory appearance at meetings now and then, just to keep up with what we're doing."

He looked so forlorn that, feeling sorry for him, Gwen reached out to put a hand on his arm.

"It's all right, really," he reassured her and gave

her hand a pat. "In the end, I want all my children to do exactly what they want to do. Somehow, you represent Arzelia to me; the Arzelia that might have decided to stay. And as subjective and irrational as it may sound, I guess that's the reason why I'm willing to take a gamble on you. Because I want so badly to win. . . ."

Gwen was touched by Phanor's explanation and felt the strong emotion behind his confession.

"I realize that at first there might be a language barrier," he went on, "and that you haven't had a lot of experience yet in cross-company negotiations, but I would be patient and give you all the time you need. And," he added, "I'm sure that we can decide on a salary that would be more than satisfactory to you."

Gwen began to stumble with a response. But Phanor raised his hand as if to halt her from speaking and said, "No, Gwen. This is a serious decision, and I don't want you to give me an answer yet. I insist that you think about it—at least overnight. Or you can take more time if you need it and even call me from the States after you get back. I'm still going to recommend you as head of the next team visit here, so in any event we will be working together again soon."

Although she still had no idea what she would do about it, Gwen was thrilled by Phanor's offer. At last, all her hard work had paid off, and she had done it on her own terms. Wouldn't Kurt be proud!

When they walked back to where Beatriz was giving the group a little tour of her prize cactus garden, Kurt looked up as Gwen approached and raised a quizzical eyebrow in her direction. I bet he would like to know what we've been talking about, she thought, and couldn't keep herself from flashing him a secretive smile. Phanor went over to Kurt and, draping his arm around his shoulder, began talking to him in low tones. When Kurt looked back at Gwen as if he were checking to make sure that she noticed Phanor's attention to *him*, Gwen was nonplussed. Was it game time again? she wondered, and walked over to where Beatriz was standing.

In the next hour the afternoon sun fell low in the sky, and with it the entire city quieted down for siesta. The group decided that it would be necessary to meet for half of the following day in order to tie up the loose ends of their business. They would take this afternoon off to work separately. Phanor called for the car that would bring them back to the Campo Bello, and everyone exchanged warm good-byes.

"*Gracias*, Señora," Gwen said to Beatriz in her best accent, and in response Beatriz kissed both her cheeks in a European-style good-bye.

"My house is your house," Beatriz said, translating the Mexican expression of friendship. Gwen was touched by the gesture, and walked to the car feeling full, content, and, most of all, successful.

"Well, that went well, I think," Kurt said as he settled himself next to Gwen and swung his arm up and over the back of the seat.

"I agree," Gwen said. "Though of course there's still some last-minute work to do, like updating some of the statistical charts to reflect the decisions we've made so far. I think we should leave copies of the basic, corrected contract for Phanor, too, so he has a model to work with after we leave."

"My, my, I'm impressed by your efficiency, Gwen," Kurt responded, but not without an edge of sarcasm in his voice. They were sitting so close together that she could feel the heat of his body and smell the faint, spicy cologne he wore. As he spoke he let his knee drift over and rest against her leg.

"You certainly have made things easy for me on this trip," Kurt went on. "You've taken over negotiations like a real pro, and are still cranking out the work. And to think that I thought I needed Connie."

Gwen turned her head to look at Kurt. "I hardly think that my job has any relationship whatsoever to what Connie would have done. I did the job that was assigned to me, and anything beyond that was just taking up the slack for those who weren't as well prepared." If he was going to be sarcastic, she could be too.

"Oh, I don't know if I would exactly call it slack," Kurt retorted. "It seems that Phanor simply took a stronger liking to you than to me. When you hold court with the boss in the garden, Gwen, you know that you're just going to have to be responsible for the outcome, even if it means extra work."

"As a matter of fact," she responded to his barb, "my conversation with Phanor in the garden was personal, and had nothing to do with the merger." The tension inside the car was mounting, and Gwen squirmed uncomfortably in her seat.

"Oh, don't get the idea that I mind your friendship with Phanor, or that I'm questioning the quality of your work, Gwen." The seriousness in his voice told her that he might, finally, be getting to the heart of what was bothering him. "It was very astute of you to figure out beforehand that you were being considered for the trip, and to come so well equipped with *volumes* of backup material. But," he continued, "everyone knew that Phanor was the one who called Tonkan down here for the meeting and that the whole merger plan was in the bag before we got here. The point I'm making is that there is no great reward for overachievement in the area of public relations. Any work taken on that's above and beyond the call of duty, any lone-star performances, can be interpreted as individual horn blowing for personal gain. And doesn't make for good teamwork," he concluded, and sat back in his seat.

"Well, maybe you're right," Gwen said, and turned to peer out the window, doubts about her own behavior rising in her mind. Perhaps she had been trying too hard—though she certainly hadn't had the impression that the merger was a foregone conclusion. But as the car sped along, she realized that what Kurt had said could not be entirely true. After all, Phanor hadn't acted as if he was so sure of the deal before they had given their presentations. And she had never, in her entire life, been accused of monopolizing the limelight. . . .

Kurt interrupted her thoughts when he pulled

her head down to rest on his shoulder. "Oh, darling," he said, "please don't brood over what I said. I *am* proud of your good work. Really!" He kissed her forehead. "And I even have a little surprise for you. I've arranged to rent a car for the afternoon to go out and visit a friend who runs a sort of hacienda just outside of town. It's just far enough out to give us a quick look at the country-side, and a few hours out of the city. We'll slip out quietly, and no one will even miss us. How about it?" he asked as he put a hand under her chin and turned her face up so that he could see her.

Gwen thought for a moment about her plan to corner him and talk but she told herself they could do that anywhere. It would be wonderful to get out of the city and see more of Mexico. "Do you really think we should?" she asked, and instantly answered her own question with a "Yes, I'd love to go. I'll have to stop by my room and change. We'll need bathing suits. And towels too?"

"Yes," Kurt said. "Nothing too formal. But we may not make it back for dinner, so bring a change of clothes, too. I'll meet you in the hotel lobby in half an hour," he said, and Gwen raced off to her room to change.

As she packed her canvas shoulder bag with her bathing suit, towel, and other things she would need, Gwen thought happily that this would be the first day she was able to spend with Kurt. Now that their business meetings were over, the carefree woman in her emerged and relished the long afternoon and evening they would be together.

"My lover," she said out loud, and was startled by the strange sound of the words.

Gwen changed into a simple, white sundress. Today she was going to have fun. And it was as simple as that!

Chapter Six

From the moment Gwen was seated beside Kurt in the little compact car, she was glad she had agreed to come along. As beautiful as the Campo Bello was, at moments during the conference it had come to feel like a prison. She felt a sense of freedom as the car wove its way through the city toward the outskirts of town. Kurt increased the speed when they finally turned onto what might be called a highway, and though the road was bumpy and potholed, the cool breeze on her face felt good. She sighed with contentment. Now they were in the country, and Gwen scoured the vista with her eyes, anxious to get her first look at rural Mexico.

"What's that growing?" she asked Kurt, and glanced over at the flat fields that stretched back into endless space.

"It's corn," Kurt said, "and the other is maguey."

In between the fields there were long stretches of rust-colored earth that looked untilled and barren. "Farming isn't really good here," Kurt went on. "There's already been so much land erosion, because of the droughts. And the people learned too late about things like crop rotation and irrigation." Gwen felt the concern in his voice. "But you know, even this is something that computerization can help."

Just then the sound of a honking horn interrupted their conversation. Gwen threw her hand up over the back of Kurt's seat and turned around to see what was coming.

"It's a bus," she said to Kurt, and he pulled over to the side of the road in order to let it pass. "Look at that!" she cried in amazement. "They'll never make it." She was astonished by the sight of the dilapidated bus, so loaded with people that it seemed to sag in the middle like a full belly. People were riding on the fenders, on the roof, and some seemed to be hanging on to nothing at all. To top it off, along with their children, the women were carting roosters, pigs, and even goats.

"They're probably off to market," Kurt said. He laughed when he looked over at Gwen, who sat with her mouth agape, staring after the cloud of red dust that trailed the caravan. "They'll make it," he reassured her, and pulled back onto the road.

Once back at a steady speed, Kurt looked over again and started to laugh.

"Why are you laughing?" she wanted to know.

"I guess I'm just amused by your reactions to everything here," he said, and then added, "You know, Gwen, I don't know anyone else who is as much pure *fun* to be with."

His comment caused her a moment of embarrassment. No one had ever told her that before. It was such a nice thing for him to say. . . .

"Tell me more about where we're going," she

asked in an attempt to divert the attention away
from her.

"A few years ago when I was here with some
friends, they introduced me to a woman named
Rosa who owns a hacienda about fifteen miles
north of the city. From the first moment I met her,
I found her fascinating and I spent as much time
talking to her as I possibly could," Kurt began,
and Gwen's interest was immediately aroused.

"Should I be jealous," she asked lightly.

He laughed. "Only of her cooking. We call her
Mama Rosa. She's from Madrid. She came here
with her husband in the early thirties, and they
managed to build up a regular clientele who stayed
at the hacienda. It's like a very old-style Spanish
hotel, with a courtyard, swimming pool, and just
enough modern conveniences to make it comfortable. Mama Rosa and her husband, José, had
seven children, I think. Three died when they
were small, and now she has only one daughter
left to help her. Her husband died five years ago;
I never met him. It was then that she had to
make her decision whether or not to stay here
or to return to Spain to the little family left
there."

Kurt continued to talk about Mama Rosa in glow-
ing terms, almost as if, Gwen thought, Mama
Rosa were truly his mother. It was strange: she
had never heard him speak of his own family.

Then the landscape around them changed again,
distracting her. Signs of vegetation reappeared,
and Gwen saw the silhouette of houses in the
distance. They were approaching what looked like
a small village. Kurt turned off onto a side road,

and within a matter of minutes he swung into the driveway of Mama Rosa's.

The hacienda looked so ancient that it took on a mysterious, remote air. Yet there were several cars parked in the driveway. Gwen got out of the car and took a deep breath of the fresh country air. She sensed a feeling of hospitality, and began to understand how guests whose business was in the city might decide to drive the few extra miles to spend their nights there.

At that moment a short, plump, black-haired woman come out from a corner room off the large, circular courtyard and approached Kurt with open arms, and she knew immediately that this must be Mama Rosa.

"Hijo," the woman said warmly, and taking his face between her hands, she gave him a loving kiss. A white apron covered her simple black dress, and Gwen saw that it was only her large girth that kept her from being a real beauty. Her long hair, pulled severely back from her face in a bun at the back of her neck, framed a classical Spanish face that reflected not only pride but also warmth and humor.

"How are you?" Kurt asked, and almost lifted the woman off her feet in an affectionate hug. "I've just finished my business in Guadalajara and I've come for a swim," he said, and she beamed up at him in response. Kurt turned to Gwen, and introduced her. "This is my good friend and colleague, Gwen Franklin."

"Hello," Gwen said, and stepped forward. The woman before her was so solid, so real, that it made her feel a little superficial in comparison.

"Hola," Mama Rosa said, and squeezing Gwen's hand, she garnished her gesture with a broad smile that immediately captured Gwen's heart and secured her friendship. Gwen gave Kurt an I-see-what-you-mean look, and he winked back at her.

"So," said the woman, "you have come for a little rest after your hard meetings. Here, let me show you to a room where you can change. The pool is yours, and I will send Carmen out with a little refreshment for you in a while. It makes me happy you never forget me, Kurt," she said, and taking his arm she showed them to a room which opened off the short end of an L-shaped line of doors that were a part of the maze of hallways leading back to the courtyard and to the glistening swimming pool at the far end.

"Here we are," said Mama Rosa, and opened the door to what was obviously a bedroom.

"Thank you, Rosa," Kurt said, and again hugged the woman before she bustled off.

For a moment, Gwen wondered why they had not been shown to separate rooms. Had Kurt explained in advance, or had he done this so many times before that Rosa took the arrangement for granted? Nonsense, she told herself. Rosa probably trusts him to observe the proprieties. And in any case, what he did in the past has no relation to *us.*

The question of the room resolved, Gwen inexplicably felt a surge of shyness at the idea of changing in front of Kurt. It wasn't as if he hadn't already seen her naked. She felt ridiculous when she saw that he had noticed her hesitation.

"The room is only for changing into our suits

and for parking our things," he said. "Rosa is generous enough to let us use it for the afternoon. Why don't you go in first. I'll wait outside and change after you."

"Thanks," Gwen said, smiling at him. When he wanted to, she thought, Kurt could be very considerate. She stepped inside and closed the door behind her. After she had pulled on her new bathing suit, she caught a glimpse of herself in the cabinet, and stopped, a bit shocked. She hadn't remembered the bathing suit as being so revealing. Well, she thought wryly, it's too late now, and gathering up her towel, her suntan lotion, and her dark glasses, she stepped outside.

"Nice," Kurt said in a low voice as he boldly looked her up and down. "Very nice. Why don't you go on ahead and find us two comfortable chairs facing the sun. I'll be along in a minute." Gwen took the order and started for the pool.

Oh, it was all so glorious, she thought as she threw her towel over the back of the lounge chair and sat down and stretched out her long legs. Within seconds the hot sun was drawing out little drops of perspiration across her forehead, baking the tiredness and strain from her muscles.

"Comfortable?" she heard Kurt ask as he came up alongside her. He pulled his chair slightly closer to hers so that when he lay down their arms were almost touching.

"It's wonderful"—she sighed—"but very warm. We'll have to watch ourselves or we'll be burned to a crisp."

"We'll keep an eye on one another." He cast a long, lingering look down the length of her shapely legs. "If I start looking like a lobster, just holler. I'll do the same for you. Meanwhile, we have the water to keep us cool."

"Yes," Gwen murmured back, and closing her eyes, she turned a worshipful face to the sun. She felt its penetrating rays seep into every pore and warm her entire body, and she let out a sigh of contentment.

When she opened her eyes a few minutes later, she saw that Kurt seemed to have dozed off. A stray impulse told her to take advantage of the moment and steal a secret look at his long, lean body as it lay covered with a fine perspiration, glistening in the sun. Kurt's suit, like hers, left little to the imagination. When Gwen's wandering eyes reached his muscular thighs, she felt her pulse speed up, and she quickly averted her glance. She tried to concentrate instead on the beauty of the sun sparkling on the water, but her body's indifference told her there was no comparison.

Kurt opened his eyes just then, and looking over at her with a knowing smile, he said, "Want to go in?" He motioned toward the pool.

"Yes," she said, "I'm ready," and she stood up, shed her glasses, and running to the edge of the deep end of the pool, went into the water in a perfect dive.

Kurt followed her lead, and in a few minutes they were cutting through the water like two sleek dolphins, twisting and turning in a mock contest. Gwen had learned to swim as a young child, and had always loved the water. All the more reason, she had often thought, for living in a state like Minnesota with so many lakes. But she hadn't had a good workout in a long time, and she wanted to take advantage of the heated pool.

Leaving their play, she went to the end of the pool and started swimming laps. Back and forth, gracefully but relentlessly, she put herself through the paces she had learned, loving the sensuous feeling of the heavy yet buoyant water rushing past her, caressing her.

Out of the corner of her eye, Gwen saw that Kurt, too, was enjoying a real workout, swimming laps at such a fast pace that he had probably already counted off a couple of miles. Finally he stopped, and bracing himself up by his strong elbows on the edge of the pool, watched Gwen perform her private follies.

She was swimming more slowly than he had done, but finally she tired, too, and swimming to the opposite side of the pool to catch her breath, she clutched at the edge for support and gulped deep breaths of air until her heartbeat returned to normal. Then she put her head back and for a moment closed her eyes and relished the feeling of exhaustion.

Then she felt something like the pinch of a crab at her toe. She kicked back instinctively, and hit something big and warm. When she looked down into the water she saw a human body reflected beneath the surface.

"Kurt, don't." She laughed as he surfaced.

"Hi," he said, and propped himself up next to her. "Nice, isn't it?"

"It's heaven." She smiled at him. His golden hair was dark and slicked back by the water, and his eyes glistened in the reflected sunlight.

He reached over and pushed back a strand of maverick hair that hung over her forehead and commented, "You're a very good swimmer," and moved slightly closer to her.

"I've been doing it all my life," she answered, and looked up into eyes, only inches away from her own. At that moment her hand slipped off the slippery edge of the pool, and she began to sink.

With a graceful sweep of his arm, Kurt grabbed her around the waist so that she coud reach up and get a new hold.

"Thanks," she sputtered, tossing her hair back out of her eyes.

He smiled his response, and instead of removing his arm from her waist he pulled her toward him and closed the last few inches that separated them, so that their slippery bodies touched and their legs began to intertwine. Gwen felt a cool wet mouth descend on hers, and the effect of its touch made her go limp in his arms. She was unable to move, and even had she wished to escape, she knew she could not. Her body had already surrendered to his. His lips toyed with hers, gently nibbling, sucking, teasing them apart so that his wickedly devious tongue could insinuate itself into her mouth and twine itself around her own tongue.

"Oh," she cried out when Kurt reached over and effortlessly slipped his hand inside the top of her bikini. He cupped her breast in a rough caress that aroused her nipple till it became an erect little signal of her desire, then moved his hand down to caress her bottom and press her hips to his own. Gwen could feel the urgency of his desire

for her, and his evident readiness that she felt
through their wet suits made her press herself
against him in a promise that she would not deny
him entrance.

Kurt pulled away and broke their kiss, and,
panting for breath, said, "We're going to use the
room." Without another word he hoisted himself
up out of the water, then reached down for her
hands and lifted her effortlessly out to stand beside him.

Without saying a word, hand in hand, they
walked over to their chairs and collected their
belongings. Kurt had once more aroused her to a
burning intensity of sexual awareness, so that even
as she followed him across the courtyard and back
to the room she felt attuned to the sight, the
smell, the very sound of him as his strong legs
padded across the courtyard.

She heard the thud of the door as it slammed
shut behind them, and then Kurt was next to her,
pulling her into his arms. For a long moment he
held her tight, until their breathing fell into a
matched rhythm, one which accelerated when he
delivered a kiss that quickly raged out of control
and turned into a wild frenzy of biting and probing.
Wave after wave of desire washed over her, till it
seemed she could never have enough of him, never
bring his body close enough to her.

Then, with what seemed like a flick of his wrist,
he removed Gwen's bikini. Another slight motion
and he stood naked beside her, urging her over to
the bed, where they tumbled down together, never
breaking their embrace.

"Every time I'm with you I want you more,"

Kurt said in a husky voice as he clutched her to him with a fierceness he had never shown before, and Gwen knew that there was little time left for foreplay. Neither of them would wait much longer. She dug her fingers into the thick mat of blond hair that covered his chest and held on to her newly discovered anchor. But then Kurt gently extricated her hand and led it down to another forest of tangles, to the center of his desire, showing her his need for her.

All of her earlier shyness left her and a triumphant passion took it's place. It was Gwen now who guided their lovemaking, Gwen who finally brought them together, deftly, gracefully, and it Gwen who started the motion for their voyage back underwater into a world of deep intensity that sent ripples of pleasure soaring through her and broke down all of the barriers that separated them, until they became one wild, flailing, underwater creature who rode the waves of ecstasy and the violent currents of desire.

"We belong together." She heard Kurt's hoarse whisper from what seemed like a long distance away, and then, "It's never been like this before—never."

His words brought her to the edge of delirium, to the loss of control and the loss of desire for control. At that moment she wanted only to be possessed completely, and Kurt seemed to understand.

He rolled over on top of her and drove deeper and deeper into her until she reached the pinnacle of her bliss, calling out his name, a clear cry of happiness in the tiny room. At the same second

Kurt shuddered wildly against her, their echoing pleasure multiplying the experience beyond anything Gwen had ever felt. At last, they slowly floated back to consciousness and punctuated their lovemaking in a last, ritualistic kiss.

"I don't think I've ever felt so good," Kurt whispered against her hair, and Gwen shook her head in agreement. She lay resting on his chest, her senses seemingly heightened as she listened to the loud pounding of his heartbeat and breathed in the musty perfume of their lovemaking. More than anything, she wanted to drop off to sleep, to stop this moment and turn it into a dream she could savor for a long, long time. But Kurt moved slightly so that he could see her face, and when she opened her eyes she could tell that he wanted to talk.

"Where did you learn to make love like that?" he asked tenderly.

"You've taught me everything I know," she answered, and he leaned over and gave her another quick kiss.

"I've never met anyone as beautiful as you, in every way," he said seriously. "Or anyone who fits against me so perfectly."

Gwen didn't know whether to laugh or cry at the silly poignancy of his words.

"It seems as if we've found a pretty good fit," she replied, and didn't know how to go on. It was strange that her body had known instinctively what to do and how to respond to their lovemaking. But in the quiet conversation that followed, she felt inexperienced and even a little awkward.

"And it'll get better with practice," Kurt mumbled, and propped himself up on his elbow. "You are adorable after you make love," he said, and lay his hand on her flat stomach.

"And you are . . ." She couldn't find the right word to explain the gentle softness that shone in Kurt's eyes without sounding melodramatic or sloppily sentimental. "Devastating!" she said, and gave him a quick hug.

Gwen looked at Kurt and felt a deep surge of feeling. A feeling, she finally let herself realize, that had been with her since their first night together, a feeling that could only be love.

"Speaking of good things," he said, abruptly shifting their mood, "I'm starving. Aren't you?"

"Yes." She giggled. "Our, ah, exercise had made me ravenous."

"You stay right there," he insisted. "Don't move an inch. I'm just going to run out and find Carmen. I'm sure she's got something ready by now."

When he left the room, Gwen lay back to enjoy the thought that she was the luckiest woman on earth. She had finally found someone to fill the lonely, empty void in her life, someone who would warm her bed at night and make her whole.

Still, she thought as she closed her eyes in an effort to concentrate even harder, she knew so little about him. Where was he born? she wondered, and what was his family like? And even more importantly, what were his expectations for their relationship? What would happen when they got back to reality; back to the day-to-day routine life at Tonkan?

Gwen heard a click at the door, and Kurt burst into the room carrying a large tray. "Violà, madame," he said as he sauntered over to the bed and put it down on the table. The plates on the tray were loaded with fresh fruit and three kinds of cheese, and alongside the cheese lay a loaf of fresh, homemade bread. Gwen stared at it happily; as much as she liked Mexican food, she was finally tiring of tortillas.

Kurt reached for the bottle of red wine, uncorked it, and poured out two large glasses. "To you, my darling," was his toast, accompanied by a sensuous kiss.

"To us," Gwen seconded, and hungrily attacked the food.

"Hey, wait for me!" Kurt laughed when he saw the rapacious look in her eyes. "For such a skinny thing, you certainly have a huge appetite."

"Skinny! Who are you calling skinny?" She punched his shoulder, then started piling food on her plate. "Anyway, if I'm hungry it's your own fault." She dropped a kiss on his muscular thigh. *And to think that just a few moments ago I felt shy*, she thought.

"You know what's going to happen again if you keep that up, don't you?" Kurt said. "I'm going to tickle you."

He started to reach toward her sensitive waist, and she quickly exclaimed, "Time out!" She put a pat of cheese on the heel of the bread, and started eating. For the next few minutes, there was silence as she and Kurt sat side by side, picnicking on their bed in the small, whitewashed room.

When they were finally done, when there was not a crumb of food left on their plates, Kurt gulped down the last of his wine and stared at

Gwen with a look of growing satisfaction in his black eyes. He moved toward her and, putting an arm around her shoulders, pulled her down next to him on the bed.

"I feel so lazy," Gwen murmured, and closed her eyes. All of her physical needs were satisfied, and she was moving closer and closer to sleep.

"Did you know that you've got the most enchanting dimple . . . right here?" Kurt whispered, and kissed a spot on her shoulder.

"No." Gwen opened her eyes, lazily watching his full, sensuous lips.

"And there's another one over here," he said, and touched his lips to her other arm. "Stick with me, kid, and you'll find out all kinds of new things about yourself." He let his hand fall to her breast.

"I can tell you something about yourself, too," Gwen teased back.

"What's that?"

"On second thought I don't think I'm going to tell you," she said.

That of course provoked a wrestling match that ended with the bed in total disarray and Gwen flat on her back, her hands pinned at her sides, and Kurt straddling her supine form.

"Tell me," he demanded. "If you don't talk, you'll have to suffer the consequences," he warned with a lascivious smile.

"Well." Gwen tried to look as if she were making a difficult decision. "Okay, I'll tell you." She pulled his ear down to her mouth and whispered, "You're the best-looking, most exciting, and sexiest man I have ever met." Her bold outburst made her blush, and Kurt's smile broadened when he saw her embarrassment.

She waited breathlessly for his kiss. When he pulled her to him and their mouths met, they shared a long, communicative exchange that spoke of their mutual happiness and deep satisfaction.

"You are so wonderful," Kurt said seriously when he finally broke away. He seemed to be searching for something hidden deep within her eyes. "Gwen," he started again in a faltering voice, "I want to talk about what's going to happen when we get back."

"Get back?" Gwen at first didn't understand. "You mean back to Minneapolis?"

"Yes," he said. "When we get back to Minneapolis. Now that I've finally found you, you don't think I would ever let you get away again, or even out of my sight for an instant, do you?"

"Don't worry, I'm not going anywhere." She felt flattered by his concern, but a tone of possessiveness in his voice made her suddenly nervous. She sat up in bed alongside him. Maybe he needed reassurance, she thought, and said, "I expect that when we get back to Minneapolis we'll make love again, only in a colder climate. I, myself, am sure that it wasn't the sun that was the cause of all of this debauchery." She laughed in an attempt to keep the mood light.

"I can't wait," he said. "You'll be delicious on those long, winter nights, snowbound in some cabin on a remote northern lake."

Kurt beamed Gwen an intimate smile. She could see his relief at knowing that their relationship would continue when they got home. But her elation was quickly extingushed when she remembered the job offer from Phanor and thought about all of the ramifications that went with it.

"Kurt," she began slowly, "there's something I've got to tell you."

"What is it?" he was suddenly attentive. "Don't tell me you have a John Doe waiting for you back home?"

"No. There's no John Doe back home. But those long, cold winter nights may be entirely over for me if I take the job with Phanor," she said. At the expression on his face she desperately wished she could recall the words, rephrase them and surround them with mollifying explanations.

"Job? What job?"

"Phanor wants me to join his firm here in Mexico. It would mean a promotion and a raise," Gwen said.

Kurt pulled himself up straighter and gave her a long, blank stare. His face registered confusion, and he stuck out his chin. "Well, it's a shame that you won't be able to accept it. Not after all that's happened between us . . ."

Gwen looked back at him but said nothing, and Kurt reached out and pulled her into his arms in a tight hold. "Not unless you want to take me with you." His attempt to hide the strain in his voice failed.

For a moment Gwen was too startled to answer. Then, trying to sound calm, she said, "Kurt, this is a serious job offer, a very good one . . ."

Before she could finish, he interrupted. "Of course it is, and I'm proud of you. They'd be lucky to have you. But you've got just as good a future at

Tonkan. And since we both have jobs there—Gwen, I'm not telling you to stop working. . . ."

This time it was Gwen who interrupted, as she felt a familiar anger rush through her. "Damn straight you're not telling me—you don't *tell* me anything."

"Gwen." He too was clearly angry, but he addressed her in a sweetly reasonable tone. As if, she thought, he's talking to a cranky child. "Gwen, I'm sorry—you know what I meant. Do you really want a commuter marriage?"

"Marriage?" Gwen couldn't believe her ears. "What are you talking about?"

"Marriage, Gwen." He was no longer trying to hide his anger. "You know. White dress, house in the suburbs, double bed, eventually children. What did you think this was leading to, anyway, a long-term keep-it-hidden affair? I thought we had something special!"

"We do!" She was close to tears now. How could she explain? It had been so right, and now it was all going so wrong. "But Kurt, my career is very important to me. You know how hard I've worked. And now without even considering this offer, or discussing our options—the idea of you relocating isn't just a joke, you know—you tell me to refuse it. And what's more, you've got me barefoot and pregnant in the kitchen before you've even asked me to to marry you. *Asked* me Kurt, not told me." She felt her body ache with disappointment. It was as if the happiness that moments before had been so real was about to vanish before her eyes.

She stopped for a moment to glance at Kurt. He

looked so truly miserable that she made an attempt to control her anger. "Kurt, there have been
problems between us since we first met, but I
always believed that we would resolve them, be
together."

"On your terms." He spat the words out in an
icy rage. "This isn't a business merger. You don't
sit down and make charts, or negotiate percentage
points. I'm talking about love, Gwen. A life and a
home together. And apparently you've become
such a cold-blooded, ambitious career woman that
you think you can live happily without it!"

"If it's love you're so suddenly interested in,
why don't you quit *your* job and come with me to
Mexico instead of just assuming that I'll turn down
Phanor?" Gwen lashed back at him.

"And I suppose that this wonderful raise of
yours will support us both?" he yelled.

"As well as your job at Tonkan." The moment
she said the words, she knew she had ended their
discussion, but even if she hadn't known, the
expression on his face would have told her.

She snatched up her clothes, ran into the bath-
room, and slammed the door behind her. Grab-
bing for the sink, Gwen held on for a moment,
overcome by sheer physical exhaustion. She dressed
quickly, and prayed that she would have the stamina to make it back to the hotel. Pain was building
up in a wall of tears behind her eyes that inter-
fered with her vision and threatened to break
through the fragile veneer she still maintained.

Gwen walked out into the bedroom and saw
thankfully that Kurt was already dressed and had

even collected his things. She hastily grabbed her suit off the floor and jammed it into her canvas bag. They left the hacienda in total silence.

The ride back to the Campo Bello seemed to take an eternity, and Gwen kept thinking that there must be something wrong with the ventilation in the car. She was having trouble breathing, as if there wasn't enough oxygen in the air.

At times she inadvertently caught glimpses of Kurt's face, and she could see that along with the anger, he was hurt, just as she was. It seemed as if the violent rupture of their relationship had left him, as it had her, in a state of shock. She turned her head back to the front and began counting off the long minutes it would take to get back to the hotel.

When they finally arrived, she felt more tired than angry and, taking her things out of the car, turned, out of habit, to say good-bye. But Kurt was clutching the wheel with white knuckles, staring straight ahead, so she spun around and walked inside, wanting only the solace of her own room and time alone to collect herself.

It was early evening by the time she propped herself under the shower, hoping that the hot sprays of steaming water would wash away her grief. She decided against any dinner and instead busied herself with packing. They were leaving early the next day, and she wanted to be ready.

Gwen closed her suitcase and climbed into bed, but the minute her head hit the pillow she knew that she wouldn't be able to sleep. Instead she let the day's events play in her head in a rerun of pain and pleasure so intermingled that she was over-

come by the irrationality of it all. She was sure
that in some way the shattering end to her love
had permanently damaged her. Finally she buried
her face in her pillow and began to cry.

How long she cried, she wasn't sure. But when
she looked up again, some time later, she knew that
she had come full circle. Every last tear of expecta-
tion was expunged, the bitter ones that had stuck
in her throat and threatened to choke her. Gwen
felt her anger break down and dissolve in her
salty tears, letting her breathe freely. As she pulled
down the covers and climbed back into bed she
feld oddly numb, and knew that she would sleep.

In the morning, it was the sound of the tele-
phone and the announcement of breakfast that
woke her from her slumber. Gwen rose, lethar-
gically, and prepared to meet the day.

Once downstairs, she picked at the food on her
plate with her fork instead of eating; she wasn't
hungry. When she looked up and saw Kurt walk
into the restaurant her heart began to beat faster,
but she tried to ignore his entrance. He sat down
alone, at a table across the room from hers. In a
stolen glance at his downcast face, she noticed the
dark circles that lined his eyes and felt a stab of
something close to sympathy. But one cold stare
from Kurt and she immediately hardened.

When the limousine that was to take them to
the airport drove up, Gwen asked the driver, "I
wonder if it would be possible for me to ride in
front? I've seen so little of the city."

"No problem," said the driver. "It's not against
regulations."

Gwen put down her suitcases by the edge of

the curb and sank tiredly into the front seat. Kurt got in the back several minutes later, without even looking at her. As the car pulled out she breathed a sigh of relief at having separated herself, at least temporarily, from the other passenger.

Chapter Seven

~

"I don't know, Betty. Maybe I acted too harshly."

"I disagree," Betty said firmly. "When Kurt just assumed that you'd abandon the Mexican job, he proved that he's never going to take your career seriously. No matter what he says, he's always going to compete with you and he expects to win. In fact, he expects you to let him win—or not even compete."

Gwen looked at her roommate through a veil of fatigue.

"Look, Gwen," Betty said. "Why don't you sit down and try to relax. I'm going to go out to the kitchen and make us a cup of tea. Then we'll talk more about it."

Gwen responded obediently and did as she was told. It was good to have someone look after her at a time when she needed it. She walked over to the hardwood rocker that was by far the best chair in the house for reminiscing, and she thought about the trip home.

She had managed to avoid Kurt by riding in the front seat on the way to the airport; he had avoided her during the long airplane ride by burying his head in a book. She had had no hand to hold on to when the plane took off and landed, and no one to talk her out of her nervousness during the flight. Although it took only slightly over four hours, Gwen felt as if traveling from Mexico to Minneapolis was akin to going from Earth to Mars. They landed with ease at the Twin City metropolitan airport and filed off the plane, and she was disoriented by the crowds of Nordic faces set against the midwestern topography.

After collecting their luggage, they hailed a cab and Gwen found herself sitting in the backseat beside Kurt. She inched over to the window, trying to put as much distance between them as she possibly could, but when she looked over at him he was watching her, and she quickly glanced away. She had nothing to say to him.

"All right," Kurt said. "We might as well get it over with. I can see that you would prefer to sit in the corner and pout, but you and I will still be working together tomorrow, and many days after that. I don't intend to make a spectacle of myself by having to avoid you at work, Gwen. I'm willing to forget what happened if you are, and I think we should leave it at that."

He was right, and Gwen actually felt grateful that he had approached the issue instead of letting things slide. It would be hard to work together if they had to waste energy trying to avoid one another. After all, what happened between them was now history. All they had to do was return to their roles as business associates.

She told him as much. "Don't worry about me, Kurt. I won't give you any trouble at the office and will never again refer to what happened, and I ask you to do the same."

Gwen thought she noticed a hint of dejection in Kurt's eyes when he responded, "Fine," and then looked back to the front, indicating that as far as he was concerned, the conversation had ended.

"Right here," Gwen said to the driver when they reached her house and she began to gather her things. Kurt got out, too, and helped Gwen remove her suitcases from the trunk and carry them to the door.

"I'll see you at work tomorrow then . . . Miss Franklin," Kurt had said when he turned to leave, in a mock rehearsal for the following day.

Gwen recognized a cue when she heard one, and she responded. "Fine." Still, she couldn't let the script end on that line.

"But Kurt," she said. She looked up and their eyes met. "My name is still Gwen."

It was a great exit, but after Kurt walked off, Gwen had gone into the house and burst out crying. Betty had found her when she came out of her room to welcome Gwen back.

"Hot tea anyone?" Betty's voice broke through her reverie, and Gwen stopped rocking for a moment to still her thoughts and plant herself back in the present.

"Oh, that looks wonderful," Gwen responded, eyeing the tea and the lemon pie that went with it.

After the women had filled their cups and had settled back in their chairs, Betty resumed the conversation. "Gwen," she said, "I can't tell you how sorry I am about what happened in Mexico."

Gwen had given her a sketchy account of the incident with Kurt. "Who would have thought that he would turn out to be such a selfish, unreasonable man," Betty growled. "And to think that I even encouraged you to go out with him."

"Oh, Betty. It's not your fault. I guess I was bound and determined to get involved with Kurt, regardless of the consequences. But I didn't expect that it would all happen so fast . . . or that it would end so soon." The combination of disappointment and fatigue had sent Gwen skidding into a depression.

"How could he be so egotistical that he would actually take it for granted that you would marry him? That's the part that I can't understand," said Betty. "It isn't as if Kurt is so much older, or that he's a product of another generation. Nobody just *assumes* that marriage automatically follows an involvement these days. And in my opinion, it often isn't the best solution anyway," Betty reverted back to her role as social scientist.

"I don't know," Gwen answered honestly. "All I really can remember is feeling, suddenly, as if he had taken control of my entire life, and it scared me."

"Oh! The whole thing makes me so angry," Betty stormed. "I'd like to get my hands on that insensitive, conceited—"

"Betty. It's all right, really," Gwen interrupted her. "Besides," she spoke with new rationality, "Kurt isn't all that bad; I'm sure part of his behavior was brought on by the intensity of our relationship. . . ."

"I think you did the right thing, Gwen, and

although it's going to be hard, I know that you'll forget about him soon. But you mustn't spend as much time in the evenings alone as you did before you left. Come out with me. There are so many men who would fall all over you if you would just give them the chance."

"I really am not all that interested in meeting anyone else right now," Gwen replied. "With my luck, I'd get involved in a mess like this—or something worse—all over again. Don't worry, Betty. I'll be all right. Honest." She tried for an encouraging smile, but when she felt the tightness around her mouth and the pressure behind her eyes that could only mean pent-up tears, she knew that she was convincing no one. Gwen was going to be miserable until she got completely over Kurt—if she ever did.

Later, after taking a long walk around the lake, Gwen fell into bed and slept, and although she woke up once in the early evening, when she looked around and realized that she was in her own bed, secure in the comfort of her own home, she slipped back into the solace of deep sleep.

The following morning she felt refreshed, and after a light breakfast she gathered her things and headed out the door. As usual, she would walk to work.

It was a three-mile hike from her apartment to Tonkan, and she had devised a route that took her around Lake Minnetonka. Before Gwen moved to Minneapolis, she thought that the ten thousand lakes Minnesota boasted of was a gross exaggeration. But after a few trips through the lush state she saw that it was, in fact, studded with lakes of all shapes and sizes, even in the midst of its largest city. And Lake Minnetonka was one of the loveliest.

As she strolled along this morning, Gwen thought about the treacherous cold of the winter, and how on a couple of mornings she had been tempted to take a bus. But always, just at the point that she thought she could stand no more, something of interest would catch her eye, and she would keep on.

But now, spring had come to stay, without a doubt. She was going to enjoy her walks to work, she thought, as she strolled up to the dark green, dilapidated newsstand to pick up the morning paper.

"Good morning," Gwen said to the paper vendor.

"I wondered what happened to you," the old man behind the stand said to her. She bought the *Tribune* from him almost every day, and they had become friendly.

"I was away for a while," she replied, and handed over her quarter. "Beautiful day, isn't it?" she said, looking up into the clear, blue sky.

"Yes. It's a nice day all right," he said, and she felt like hugging him when he flashed her his familiar, toothless smile. She knew that she could never go away for very long; she simply couldn't live without seeing her paper vendor.

As usual, Gwen arrived at the office before anyone else, and took her time settling back into her old routine. Her desk was stacked with paperwork, and she let out a groan when she saw all that she had to take care of.

Gwen had planned to spend the entire day at her desk, burrowed in material that had to be written about the Mexican merger. Instead she spent most of the morning talking with other people in the office who welcomed her back and wanted to hear about the trip. She had forgotten how much she liked the people at Tonkan, and how much fun her job could be. Before she knew it, the lunch hour had arrived, and she hadn't even begun to work seriously. Then, just before she was about to step out for a breath of fresh air and a quick sandwich at the deli, she saw Kurt amble in and weave through the maze of desks to his office. Even doing something so mundane, he's graceful, she thought with a pang of loss.

When Gwen looked up again, she saw that Connie was following Kurt like a shadow. She's still waiting on him, Gwen thought, and then turned back to her desk to reread the office memorandum that announced a meeting to be held in several days. One of the points of business to be discussed was the result of the meetings with officials from Productos Mexicanos. Kurt probably hadn't been sleeping in that morning, after all, Gwen thought, but had no doubt been discussing the Mexican negotiations with his boss, the vice-president of Tonkan.

Turning her thoughts back to the business at hand, she saw that if she were going to have time for lunch, she would have to rush. She hurriedly grabbed for her coat and purse and walked briskly toward the elevator. But it was all a pretense. She didn't feel brisk, and she certainly didn't feel hungry.

Gwen was frantically busy in the days preceding the meeting, and she found that her workload allowed her to avoid and sometimes even forget Kurt—and Connie. The day of the meeting she entered the room where the meeting was to be held and found herself sitting next to Connie. Gwen greeted her warmly, and inquired after her family, and was pleased to hear that all was as well as could be expected.

"It's nice to have you back," said Connie. "How was Mexico?"

"It's nice to be back," Gwen responded. "Though Mexico is an incredibly beautiful country."

"That's what I've heard. I'm so sorry that I couldn't go with you. But Kurt told me that negotiations went well?"

"Oh yes," Gwen said confidently, and then turned her attention to Charles Norman, the vice-president of the company, who took the floor and began to speak.

"I would like to commend our representatives for their excellent work on this assignment and for their extremely successful negotiations with our Mexican friends. The result is a full-scale merger, with their company making use of our machines until they can go into production for themselves."

The people in the audience voiced their approval with a loud round of applause.

"Now I want to do something rather unorthodox that relates to our success in Mexico. As a result of the meetings there, it has become clear to all of us at Tonkan that we have an extremely talented and dedicated employee among us who had a lot to do with the Mexican acceptance of our proposal. In response to all of her hard work, I would like to announce publicly the promotion of Miss Gwen Franklin to associate vice-president and to tell her that since she seems willing to share her many talents with Tonkan, we have plenty of work for her to do. Miss Franklin, will you stand up?" He looked over at Gwen and gave her an encouraging nod.

Gwen was shocked when she heard Norman's words, and then her face lit up in joyful response.

"Congratulations," Connie whispered, and Gwen smiled back at her.

"Do you have anything to say?" Norman asked her.

"Why, yes." Gwen rose to shaky feet. "First of all I would like to thank you very much. I must say, this is all very unexpected. But I can assure you that I will try my best to do the job well and to be a credit to Tonkan. Also," she went on hesitantly, "I think I should add a word of appreciation to the corepresentative to Mexico, Kurt Jensen. He made it possible for me to make the trip in the first place." She looked over at Kurt, but he stared back at her with cold eyes. "Thank you all very much," Gwen concluded, and fell back into her chair.

Her coworkers applauded loudly. Never before had Gwen felt such a strong sense of family with the rest of the people at Tonkan, and when she looked around at the sea of faces that beamed good wishes in her direction, she was truly touched.

Then Norman took the floor again. "Oh, and before I forget. I also want you to be the first to know, Gwen, that along with your promotion, you'll finally be getting that office." The audience laughed, and Gwen joined in with them.

I'll bet Phanor's partly responsible for this, Gwen thought to herself when the focus of the meeting turned to other business. It seemed to her that Phanor had fallen into her life like some kind of godfather and had changed the direction of her future. Thank you, dear Phanor, she said to herself silently, and then tried to contain her excitement and force her mind back to serious issues.

When the meeting broke up, Gwen started making her way to the door when a group of friends from the office approached her and asked her to join them in the cafeteria for coffee.

"We're treating you," said Patsy, the woman who had sat next to her, and Gwen agreed happily.

As they made their way out Gwen stopped to accept a congratulatory handshake from Mr. Norman, and as she shook his hand she caught the flash of a scowl on the face of a man standing in a group nearby. There was someone in the office who obviously didn't back her promotion, she thought. When she turned in his direction to take another look, she met the icy stare of Kurt Jensen.

The force behind his glowering expression was strong enough to cause Gwen to stop for a moment, as if mesmerized by the intensity of his response. But a moment later she bounced back with healthy rage at his show of resentment.

Turning her back on him, she quickly left the room. Now Kurt and she were equals, and he no longer had any power over her whatsoever.

She walked out into the hallway. "Congratulations, Gwen," she heard someone say, and the sentiment was echoed by a chorus of voices. Gwen found herself surrounded by the group of women who worked with her in the office. They all piled into the elevator together.

"Oh, thank you," she said. "It was all so unexpected. I can't quite believe it."

"It doesn't come as a surprise to me," Patsy boomed. "I've never seen anyone work as hard as you, Gwen. And with your brains, I knew that it wouldn't be long before you were running the place."

The elevator stopped on the third floor, and one by one the people stepped off and into the large cafeteria. There, in the center of the room, one table was already set with plates and silverware, and in the middle of the table was a beautiful three-tiered chocolate cake.

"You knew!" She screamed her delighted accusation. A guilty silence followed.

"Come on, Jenny," Gwen coaxed one of her closest friends. "When did you know about my promotion?"

"Well," said Jenny, "I heard a rumor about it yesterday . . . and then Patsy came to me saying that she had caught the same bit of news flying around the office. So we just figured that it was probably going to happen." She took Gwen by the hand and led her over to the table. "Anyway, congratulations. I can't tell you how happy I am for you."

Gwen felt hot tears of gratitude spring to her eyes, and she tried to brush them aside casually, afraid that her friends might see her. They all got in line for the coffee that would go with the cake, and after a confusing few moments of passing milk and sugar and deciding who would sit where, they finally got themselves settled.

"Delicious!" Gwen declared after taking a large forkful of the rich cake. "Good thing I don't have this around every day."

"Gwen." She heard a voice from the other end of the table call her name, and she looked down at Naomi, the head bookkeeper. "Your promotion into the higher executive circle doesn't mean that you're going to quit fraternizing with us lower mortals, does it?"

Gwen stared at her with an open mouth. Surely Naomi couldn't be serious? "Well, I don't know," she began, thinking that she would teach her a lesson for asking such a question. "You know that I have to think about my image now and that I can no longer afford to engage in idle conversation with just *anyone*." She put up an affected hand and patted the back of her hair. "On the other hand, I suppose that if you really need me for something, you can always go ahead and make an appointment. . . ."

Gwen looked around and saw some of the women had actually fallen for her little act. She couldn't help but burst out laughing.

"For a minute there I didn't know if you were

kidding or not," one of her friends admitted, and
Gwen gave her a friendly poke in the ribs.

"You think for one minute that I'd let a promotion get in the way of my friendship with you?"
Gwen said emotionally, and looked around at her
friends. "This is where I started out, and this is
where I'll always stay," she said loyally, and then
added, "even though I imagine that now they're
going to work me so hard that I'll probably barely
find time to change my stockings."

At that moment Charles Norman and a group
of fellow executives filed into the cafeteria and
took a table across the room. Charles Norman
looked over in Gwen's direction and raised his
hand high in the air in a friendly hello. Gwen
nodded back at him.

"Oh look. There's Kurt," one of the woman
crooned, and several heads turned in his direction.
"Now *there's* a man if I've ever seen one," the
same woman droned on. She was obviously more
than just a little preoccupied with him.

"Just think, Gwen. You'll probably be working
with him very closely, now that you've got your
promotion. You must be pleased about that. . . ."

"Not particularly." Gwen tried to make her voice
sound casual. Of all the people she didn't want to
discuss, it was Kurt. "I don't think that we'll be
working any differently than we do now. . . ."

"Look at the suit he's wearing," said one of
the younger secretaries. "Doesn't he look just
dreamy . . . ?"

Oh, God, thought Gwen, and shifted nervously
in her chair. Do I really have to listen to this . . . ?

"Well, from what I understand, the only one

he's really tight with at Tonkan is his secretary, Connie," another woman piped in. "And the way they act together, I'd say they were working closely . . . very closely."

Gwen took another swallow of her hot, steaming coffee. She would have to change the subject, she thought. What Kurt did now was of no interest to her. Connie was welcome to him.

"Thank you all so much," Gwen said, standing up a few minutes later. "But I've got to get back before they decide to take back my promotion." The women's laughter followed her back to the elevator. When the doors opened, she almost bumped into Connie.

"Oh, Gwen," said Connie, "I'm sorry I missed your party. Kurt had a rush project . . ."

"It's okay," said Gwen.

"I'm really so happy for you," Connie said earnestly. "I was just told that I may be taking over some of your old administrative duties, so we'll be working together for a while."

"Great!" Gwen said with genuine pleasure. "There's no one I'd rather train. But you don't want to overload yourself, you know. I imagine that Kurt has your time pretty well filled as it is."

"Oh, no," said Connie enthusiastically. "He's been just wonderful lately. Teaching me all kinds of new things and encouraging me to broaden my horizons. I just love working for him," she raved.

Gwen barely recognized in this effusive woman the usually reserved Connie she had known. Kurt certainly was having a powerful effect on her. She noticed the contrast between Connie's involvement with Kurt and her own relationship with him, both personal and professional, which was definitely on the wane. And even in the face of her promotion, even after Kurt's open show of hostility, she couldn't suppress the tinge of jealousy she felt toward her ebullient friend.

Chapter Eight

❧

One month later, Gwen thought back to the day of her promotion and realized that the amount of work and responsibility that she had been asked to take on in her new position was far beyond her original expectations. The first week of her job had been spent getting settled into her new office. It was a corner room that had windows overlooking downtown Minneapolis on two sides. Since the light was good, she splurged on hanging plants, and even had two of her favorite posters framed for the walls. By the time she had all of her books unpacked and had filled her desk with papers, pens, and other paraphernalia, she felt settled in. She loved having her own office, loved being able to close the door anytime she wanted to be alone. Because of the privacy, she found that the amount of work that she was able to handle increased, and that the all-around intensity of her job at Tonkan almost doubled. She began to become acquainted with the subtleties of high-level job pressures that lurked beneath the surface of all major decision making.

Besides the increase in paperwork, Gwen was now being included in weekly meetings and regular negotiations with Tonkan's branch offices around the Midwest. In the short month since her promotion, she had already made two trips outside the state, one to neighboring Wisconsin and another to East Lansing, Michigan, where they were about to open a plant. Just as in Mexico, Gwen enjoyed successful negotiations on both of these trips, and when she returned home, she was greeted with praise from the powers that were—and more work.

By the fourth week she was overdue for a break, and one night at dinner Betty ventured a suggestion. "You've got to rest a little, Gwen. You're working much too hard. You've already gotten your promotion, and unless you think you're superwoman, you'll probably stay at this level for a few years, just like all the rest of the VPs do."

Gwen looked over at her friend and felt a spark of irritation. Even her disposition was in disrepair lately.

"I know you probably don't appreciate my butting in this way," Betty went on bravely, "but I really do want you to listen to me. It won't hurt if you level out and quit taking on more and more assignments. This is the time to consolidate what you have."

"I guess you're right, Betty. It's just that I wanted to make a good first impression. But I know I can't keep up this pace. I've promised myself that next week I'll try and slow down."

The following day Gwen decided that she would try and put her decision into practice and slow down the pace of her work. Instead of diving into the pile of problems that lay stacked up on her desk, she began to look at the items in terms of a schedule. Since everything couldn't be done today, she would simply have to put some things off. Moreover, looking at her work, she realized that much of it could be delegated to her secretary. As she walked, she began to wonder if Betty wasn't right, and if she hadn't begun to develop a kind of "superwoman complex" during the past month.

At midmorning Gwen sat back in her chair. Her neck and shoulders felt tense and stiff and she decided that a little more exercise and definitely more relaxation had to be scheduled into the new program as well. Right now, she would take a break and go down to the cafeteria for a cup of company coffee.

Once in the coffee line of the cafeteria a floor below, Gwen couldn't resist the temptation to grab a luscious-looking sweet roll. She ended up performing a juggling act in front of the elevator, trying to press the button without dropping either her purse or the coffee.

"Allow me," said someone from behind her as he came to her rescue by reaching over her shoulder and pressing the "up" button.

"Oh, thank you," she said. She turned to smile at her rescuer and froze. It was Kurt.

Although she had occasionally spoken to him in the office, it had been awhile since she had seen him. He looks worn out . . . thin! she thought. In a flash insight, she realized that even though he presented the picture of patience and cool control to the outside world, the pressure affected him as much or more than anyone else. For the first time she felt a touch of empathy for his position.

"How are you?" He asked the perfunctory question as though he meant it.

"Oh, I've been okay," she responded, and watched the doors of the elevator slowly ease shut.

"And how does it feel to be an associate vice-president?" Gwen's defenses rose to the front lines; the thought that, as usual, he was going to try and give her a hard time. But then he added with genuine interest, "Do you like it?"

She thought for a moment before she answered. "Yes. I think I can say by now that I like it. It certainly has brought me a long way from where I was as an administrative assistant. Some days I think I'll never get through."

"I know. They work a new one pretty hard," he said sympathetically. The doors opened up on their floor and they walked out together. "I hear that they've already got you traveling."

"Yes," she answered. It was so nice to talk with someone who really knew what her job was like. "I like it, but it wears on you."

"Let me give you a little tip," Kurt said, leaning his head down close to hers as they walked across the office. The smell of his subtle, spicy scent triggered her memory. "Don't agree to go every time they want to send you somewhere." When they reached her door, they stood outside talking.

"I tried to make every trip they wanted me to go on when I was first promoted, and it almost killed me. Now I've learned that they'll ask for the world from us all, but that we've got to agree to only what we can handle. There's a burnout point

in every business, you know, and I hope you aren't
letting yourself get too close to it."

Gwen hung on his words. This was important
information that she needed to know, and none of
her other colleagues had bothered to tell her. Wasn't
it ironic that Kurt had been the one to take the
time and clue her in, she thought, and then said,
"I really appreciate your telling me these things.
No one really showed me the ropes when I took
over. It really helps to talk to someone who knows
the job instead of having to learn every little thing
the hard way—by myself."

"I know, Gwen," he said, and she wondered
if this was the same person she had known pre-
viously. "I owe my debts to people who helped
me out. If you have any questions, let me know.
After all, you're the one who showed me the light
and made me change my attitude about Connie—
it's the least I can do. Since I realized how bright
she is, I've started involving her in projects I'm
working on, and it's made my life a hundred per-
cent easier. In fact, for starters, I'd be happy to
take a look at your recommendation on the Johnson proposal. I did some of the preliminary ground-
work on that project. If you think it would help," he
added, showing a new consideration that Gwen
had never witnessed in him before.

"Thanks, Kurt," she said before he walked off.
"I'd like that."

Gwen walked into her office and sat down at
her desk. She was amazed by the conversation
that had just taken place. Kurt had relieved an
enormous amount of her anxiety over how she
was going to accomplish everything Tonkan seemed

to want her to do, and he had done it tactfully and sensitively. Could he actually have changed as a result of their argument? Was there even a chance . . . No! She would not let herself hope. They had regained their old friendly camaraderie. That was enough.

She pulled out the Johnson file that Kurt had mentioned and decided to go over it immediately. She would go to his office with her recommendations later that afternoon and follow up on their new, open line of communication.

Two hours later, in the early afternoon, Gwen closed the file. She had digested all of the reading she had done on the project and was clear about how she thought procedures should be handled, but it was a complicated and exciting project, and she was anxious to speak to Kurt about it.

When she got to his door, she noticed that it was slightly ajar. "Kurt?" she said softly as she stuck her head inside. There, before her startled eyes, were Kurt and Connie, standing together in the middle of the room, wrapped in a tight hug.

"Excuse me," was all she could find to say. She turned quickly to leave the room.

"Gwen." Kurt hurried to stop her. "Don't go." His commanding voice compelled her to turn back to him. "I was just congratulating Connie on her promotion," he said, beaming. "You're looking at the new assistant office manager, who's going to keep us all organized for a change."

Gwen smiled and said, "How wonderful. Congratulations, Connie. I'm really happy for you." She didn't try to analyze the sudden wave of relief that washed over her. After all, she no longer had any claim on Kurt. . . .

"Thanks, Gwen," Connie said appreciatively. "I'm aware of all you've done to help me, and I want to thank you for it."

"Me too, Gwen," Kurt added. "Thanks for helping straighten me out about this young woman's capabilities." He looked over at Connie with a warm, broad smile, and Gwen flinched. Was it possible that something more intimate was going on between them? Had her first startled reaction when she looked through the door been the right one?

Kurt walked over to the new automatic coffee maker that was on a table beside his desk and poured out three cups of coffee. "I want you to know that I made this," he said, handing a cup to Gwen.

"You don't say," she said, smiling gamely, and took a sip. "Mmmm, not bad."

"To your continued success." Kurt raised his cup in a mock toast and turned to Connie.

"Thanks, Kurt. I couldn't have done it without you," Connie said, looking intently at Kurt. Gwen felt like a third wheel as she watched the two exchange a long, communicative glance. She noticed for the first time how attractive Connie was, with her light blond hair and round, pixie features. Kurt, she imagined, must have seen this long ago. She wondered why he had waited so long to extend their relationship into something personal.

"I think I'd better be getting back." Gwen finished her coffee and turned to leave. As she walked back to her own office her heels made sharp, clicking noises that played counterpart to the quick beating of her heart. She was consumed by a feeling of disappointment and felt the hurt well up from inside her. It's not as if I didn't have my chance with Kurt, she tried to rationalize her pain away. But he had been another man then. And things might have been different if he had shown the kind of regard for her that he seemed to have for Connie . . . or if Gwen had known then how much he could change. . . .

Standing alone in her office, gazing out the maze of buildings on the busy street below, Gwen felt alone, abandoned. All of the stamina she needed to maintain her strong professional front seemed to leave her. She would have to give up the idea of having any kind of romantic involvement, she finally decided, and hope that her career would be enough to keep her happy. Somehow the thought was cold comfort.

Chapter Nine

❧

Over the weekend, Gwen made an important discovery. On Sunday night, after spending the entire weekend feeling restless and lonely, trying to make catching up on chores and sleep substitute for entertainment, she faced the fact that she was lonely and that the only thing on her engagement calendar was the upcoming annual Tonkan company party.

As she sat in the living room, thinking about her dilemma, Betty walked in, plopped herself in the opposite chair, and asked, "What's wrong with you, Gwen? You don't seem to have your usual pep lately." Surprised, Gwen had nothing to say, and mistaking her silence for disagreement, Betty continued, "I think it's because you're still hung up on that egomaniac, Kurt Jensen. You've got to realize, Gwen, that he's a lost cause. In time you'll see that the whole thing was a disaster to begin with."

"Kurt's not an egomaniac," Gwen replied vehemently. That's a switch, she thought, me defending him. "He's changed, you know. He really seems like a totally different person now. . . ."

"Okay. So maybe he's wised up a little bit,"

Betty went on. "But as far as any kind of romantic involvement, you've got to quit moping around and forget about him once and for all. You told me that he's with that woman, Connie. And if she's as nice as you say she is, they may even make it all the way to the altar."

"I know," Gwen murmured. Betty, she supposed, was right. Part of the reason she had been feeling so dejected lately was that her heart refused to give up on Kurt. But it took time to get over these things, she reasoned, and during the short time they were together in Mexico, she had become deeply involved with him. Even her dreams told her that part of her was unwilling to let him go and stubbornly sent back nightly replays of the feeling of his lips on hers, or how safe she felt in the circle of his strong arms. "I *am* trying, Betty," she said. "You do know that."

"I'm not so sure," Betty answered candidly. "Why don't you ever come to parties with me, or try and meet new people? It doesn't make sense, you spending your nights alone here."

Gwen felt a surge of annoyance when she heard her roommate's words. She knew that Betty was right. But, she thought stubbornly, she wanted to start slowly, and move ahead in her own good time.

Bright and early on Monday, refreshed by her lazy weekend and armed with her new resolution, she sat at her desk, facing a huge stack of mail and another of new files.

"Don't forget about the meeting this morning," she heard someone say, and looked up to see Connie poking her head into her office.

"Hi," Gwen said. Then, "I'll be there with bells on. Thanks." She had almost forgotten about the meeting that was scheduled for that morning. She'd have to hurry if she wanted coffee beforehand. She quickly made her way down to the cafeteria.

Just as she stepped into the coffee line she saw Kurt sit down to join Charles Norman at his table. She noticed that his blond hair had grown a little bit too long, and he had a kind of haphazard look about him that she found oddly appealing. Even from across the room she could see the intensity of his piercing dark eyes as he chatted with the other men.

Gwen turned, hoping that she could get her coffee and leave without being seen. Luckily, she passed unnoticed through the line and out the door, and she breathed a sigh of relief as she walked to the elevator. This kind of intrigue at work wasn't something she handled well. She would simply have to make a greater effort to set a friendly but firm attitude toward him and get used to the idea that he was Connie's man now.

Once back at her desk, Gwen again became lost in her paperwork. Her concentration was broken by a voice that said, "Here's something I thought you might be interested in, Gwen." Kurt stood in the doorway.

Speak of the devil, Gwen thought, and said, "Thanks, Kurt." She took the file he offered her and saw that it was plump with supplemental information about the case she was working on. It would be invaluable in helping her close the deal.

"Are you all set for the big meeting?" Kurt asked her. Why were he and Connie so concerned about it? she wondered. "I'm going to argue for the construction," Kurt continued, and although she did not respond directly, she realized that she had better take another quick look at the file and make sure she knew *exactly* where she stood. This could turn into a real battle.

How strange things were getting, she thought after Kurt had left. During the past few days he had gone out of his way several times to be helpful to her. In fact, he had actually changed the entire nature of her job by slipping her information here and there that facilitated her decision making and gave her the inside scoop on what was really going on. Still, they had not had a personal conversation since the day when she had seen him with Connie. I should be glad, Gwen thought, that there's going to be no problem in developing a friendly business relationship with Kurt. But a quick glance at her watch told her it was time to turn her full attention to the file marked "Southern Michigan." She would try to explain to herself at another time why the thought of a "business" relationship with Kurt brought on a cloud of depression.

What seemed like moments later, she walked into the conference room, took a seat at the table, and looked around. All of the high-powered executives were there, including Charles Norman, looking perfectly groomed—and quite serious. Gwen glanced over at Kurt and Connie, who sat huddled together over a folder. I don't think they make such a great looking couple, she thought regretfully, no matter *what* everyone else says!

After a few moments of chaotic buzzing, the room quieted down and Charles Norman stood up to define the issue. "As you all probably know," he said, scanning the faces before him, "we're meeting here today to discuss the building of a new plant in southern Michigan under a contract that was partially supported by the federal government in an act that, hopefully, will shore up the weakening economy of the state. I believe you all have a copy of the proposal, as well as the budget that accompanies it. As you can see, this contract would not offer the company much in the way of profits. But on the other hand, we would assuredly not take any losses either. So you might say that the purpose for going ahead with the project is to promote our public image as a socially active organization. I know there's a lot of dissension on this issue, and we're just going to have to hash it all out. The floor is now open for debate," he announced, and quickly sat down.

What immediately followed seemed to Gwen more like a brawl than a civilized meeting. She had had no idea that everyone had become so personally involved in the issue, nor that their positions were based on deep-rooted political convictions.

One of the most active speakers was Kurt, who held the floor for a long time, saying that although the venture didn't promise huge profits, everyone could see that there was a no-risk equation when it came to losses. "It's about time," he said, "that Tonkan take a stand and support the blue-collar worker—and the rehabilitation of some of the

nation's most hard-hit pockets during this time of
recession. In the long run," he concluded, "Tonkan
will be seen as an innovator and a leader in the
business world and with very little effort can pull
off one of the most effective public relations cam-
paigns they have ever come up with." Kurt was
careful not to make reference to any political
implications the issue might raise, though he
spoke eloquently in defense of the bottom-line
situation.

Gwen was surprised when Charles Norman,
whom she thought had a progressive side to his
thinking, opposed Kurt and fought long and hard
to squelch the deal. By the time he had finished
delivering what she thought was a conservative
and unadventurous argument for not building the
plant, she was thoroughly involved in the case
and was in total agreement with Kurt and the
group that supported the project. Then, it was her
turn to speak.

"After listening to both sides of this debate,
there is no doubt in my mind which way Tonkan
should go," she began. She went on to give a
rousing argument for opening the plant and spoke
of the social and political benefits that Kurt hadn't
mentioned. In the end, when the vote went their
way, she knew that it was partly her recitation
that had given them the victory.

"Gwen," she heard someone at her elbow and
turned to see Kurt. The group had recessed for a
ten-minute, much-needed coffee break, and she
was trying to get a little bit ahead of the crowd so
she would have a moment to herself. "Thanks a

lot for coming to my rescue in there. I never would have gotten through to them without your help."

Gwen felt herself actually blush in response to his praise.

"You really know how to argue a case when you've made up your mind. I must say, I was very impressed," he went on, and gave her a crooked grin.

"Oh, thanks, Kurt," she said. "You're pretty good with words yourself. But in this case"—she reached for her cup and looked for a place to sit—"I really think that it's time Tonkan did get involved in public issues and showed them that they're still part of the twentieth century. I don't mind saying"—she lowered her voice and cupped her hand over her mouth so she wouldn't be overheard—"that I've seen a little bit of dead wood around here in the short time since my promotion." As soon as the words escaped her mouth Gwen wondered why in the world she had confided in him. Could she trust him? she wondered, and looked nervously in his direction.

"You don't know how many times I've thought the same thing," he replied, and Gwen let out a sigh of relief.

The coffee break seemed to fly by, and in no time everyone was settling themselves back into their chairs, ready to attack the next issue.

The second issue was one that Gwen considered to be one of her pet projects, and it involved, oddly enough, another venture of a slightly progressive and experimental nature. An entire tri-state network of school districts was interested in incorporating Tonkan's computers into their elementary and junior high school learning labs. But they wanted Tonkan to allow them the use of their machines for a preliminary study that, they felt, would be the determining factor in their decision to go ahead with the conversion. The more conservative members of the group, of course, argued that Tonkan had already done all the research necessary to display their machines and back up their sales.

Gwen felt strongly that Tonkan should go ahead with the research project and cooperate in any way they could. They were talking about big money, there was no doubt that they would make the sale, and the new research could be used in the future to strengthen their position.

She spoke at length about the benefits of cooperating with her client, but when she looked around, she could still see a great deal of skepticism on several faces. She was surprised when, after she sat down, Kurt Jensen stood up and, with the vigor of the Viking warriors of old, came to her defense. Saying that he wouldn't take no for an answer, he swept the enemy over to his side so that everyone wound up metaphorically sitting together in one neat corner. Gwen was elated, and in the end, the vote was unanimous: Tonkan would go ahead with the project.

"I guess we're even," she said to Kurt after the meeting broke up. "Thanks a lot for your help."

"You're welcome. We newcomers have to stick together against the dead wood," he said in a low voice as he walked out the door. Before she could follow him, she felt a hand detain her, and she realized that there had been someone else in the room.

"Well, well, another feather in your cap today, Gwen. You were brilliant."

"Thanks," she said, and turned around to face Charles Norman. "I'm glad the deal went through, Mr. Norman."

"How many times do I have to tell you it's Charles. We're all more or less equals at these meetings now, and it's time we dropped the formalities."

Gwen looked over at him and tried to return his aggressive smile. Standing behind the podium, he had looked taller, but now she could see that he stood only slightly above her height. She stared for a moment at the plump, gray-haired man with the innocuous blue eyes and impeccable taste in clothing, and wondered what kind of life he had outside of Tonkan.

"All right, Charles. Thanks for your kind words," she said, and turned to leave.

"Oh, and Gwen"—Charles stopped her by stepping almost directly into her path—"since we're going to be working closely together from now on, I'd like to take you out to dinner some night, just so that we can get better acquainted."

"That would be lovely. Thank you," she said.

"And of course, I'll expect a dance at the company party. You are going, aren't you?" he continued, and it was not until she agreed that he finally left.

"Whew," she said under her breath as she returned to her own office and closed the door. What is it about that man I don't like? she wondered, but just couldn't pinpoint it. She shrugged the question aside, and pulling herself up to her desk, turned back to her work.

Chapter Ten

The trip by cab to the Radisson Hotel in downtown Minneapolis took only fifteen minutes, but Gwen enjoyed every second of it. She peered out the window up into a skyful of stars that lit the way and inspired a fantasy of riding in a beautiful carriage, traveling toward a strange, new fate. As they drove around the lake Gwen noticed how the light flickered across the water and made shimmering patterns that danced in celebration of the crisp spring evening. The scent of lilacs filled the air, and she thought, how happy I am now. She realized that this was the first time in weeks that she felt free of all of her troubles, all her cares. Maybe she was finally letting go of the past, she thought, and could start to live again.

The cab pulled up in front of the hotel, and as she climbed out Gwen greeted several other Tonkan employees. She stepped into the lively scenario of downtown Minneapolis. Noisy streets, crowds of late-night diners who proudly flaunted their most fashionable attire, and neon lights that flashed on and off and made rainbow trails across the sidewalk: this was the ambience for excitement, the reason why thousands of people flocked to the great metropolis every night of the year.

It was with a pang that she left the hustle and bustle of the streets, and proceeded into the lobby. She stared up at the giant chandeliers that looked like huge, crystal earrings, tinkling their hello. The walls of the lobby were lined with huge antique mirrors, and as she passed, Gwen noticed how the light shimmered through the purple silkiness of her dress, and how sleek her figure looked in her highest heels.

"Not bad," she muttered to herself, and reached up to smooth down a stray curl.

Upstairs, she took a deep breath before stepping into the enormous ballroom that Tonkan had rented for the party and dinner. Strains of a live orchestra and the hum of conversation met her, and brought on a mood of gaiety and excitement. Reassuring herself that in the past she had always been good at parties, Gwen turned up her mouth to test a smile and walked into the room.

Once inside, someone called her name, and she turned to see Charles Norman approaching her, his hand extended in greeting.

"Gwen," he said warmly, and planted a kiss on her cheek.

"Hello," she responded formally. "I guess I'm still on time?"

"Oh yes, my dear," he said, and raised her hand to his lips. She was uncomfortable with the gesture, and stepped back to put a little more distance between them. "You know," he went on, "this night is as much a celebration of your promotion as it is of anything else."

"Oh yes," Gwen said, remembering that she should, after all, feel grateful to him. "Let me thank you again for all you did to help put it through."

"It's my pleasure, Gwen. You know how I feel about you. . . ." He looked into her eyes for a moment too long. "I think you're top-grade material, and the best we have at Tonkan."

Material? Gwen thought. Where *did* these men pick up their expressions. She replied, "Well, I certainly am going to try my best to make Tonkan proud of me," and hoped that they could now change the subject.

She allowed Charles to take her lightly by the elbow and steer her into the room and into the midst of the chattering mass of people. She looked around and saw that some of the men had brought their wives and girlfriends, but that the room was mostly filled with the men whom she worked with every day, standing around in little clusters, sipping cocktails and chatting with one another. The fact that Gwen, as a woman, was in a small minority became all too apparent, and she wondered for an instant if she wasn't altogether crazy, trying to make it against such stiff odds.

"Something to drink?" Charles said, and steered her to the bar that ran the length of an entire wall at the far end of the room.

"I'll have a glass of white wine, thank you," Gwen answered, and stepped aside so that he could order for her. She hoped that she wasn't making a mistake by letting him get her a drink. It took so little to encourage some men.

Just then she caught sight of a friend from the

office, Roger, and he started toward her. He was
with his girlfriend, Gail, whom Gwen had met
once or twice.

"Great party, isn't it?" Roger said with his usual
enthusiasm. "I hear they're gonna put the food on
soon, and that there's going to be dancing, too."

"Sounds wonderful," Gwen said just as Charles
returned with the drinks.

Gwen chatted with the three of them for some
time, but soon excused herself and walked off
alone. After all, she had come by herself, and she
was expected to mingle. So she approached a cluster
of familiar faces from work and in a short time
was involved in conversation. She was surprised
to find that these people had so little to talk about
other than the job.

Then she caught sight of Kurt walking toward
her group and felt strangely relieved. In spite of
their past encounters, she saw him as a friend.
But when a flash of bright red and then the figure
of a woman beside him came into focus, she turned
away. His date, she supposed, was Connie.

Just then dinner was announced.

"May I?" Charles seemed to appear at her side
magically, firmly taking her arm to escort her to
the table.

Gwen wasn't sure that she liked all of the attention he was showering on her and for the first
time felt vaguely suspicious of his motives. But it
would be rude to refuse him, and there was no
way to simply walk away.

"Thank you," she said, and took his arm. He
led her through the crowds and up to the buffet
table, and when she saw it she exclaimed, "How

beautiful!" The long serving table was covered with exotic platters of food from all parts of the globe. The huge assortment of meat, fish, vegetables, and colorful salads made a breathtaking sight. The colors alone, Gwen thought, were like an enormous abstract painting. And the variety of food itself was staggering.

"Where does one begin?" she asked Charles, trying to keep up a light, casual tone.

In the face of everything that was offered, the size of her plate was dwarfed, and she quickly saw that the big decision was whether to try and sample everything or to concentrate on just a couple of her favorites. In the end, she decided on the former and stepped out of line with a plate that looked like a miniature version of the big serving table.

"Let's sit here," Charles said, and led her to a table that was off a little to the side. Gwen was relieved when she saw that it was set for several people. She certainly didn't want to be separated from the rest of the group and forced to dine with him alone. They sat down and seconds later, to her relief, Roger and Gail joined them.

"Hello," Gwen once more greeted Roger and Gail and immediately turned all her attention to the amorous couple, who delved into the subject of marriage and of plans for their upcoming wedding.

"We realize that marriage seems to be a risky institution these days," Roger was saying, "but we're willing to take our chances." He drew an arm around Gail, who beamed up at him.

"I'm willing to bet my last penny that you'll go

the distance together," Gwen said, and they smiled their appreciation.

"You'll be the next to go. That I'm sure of." Roger winked at her.

"Not me," Gwen said, too quickly.

Coffee was brought to the table by waiters at the conclusion of the meal. She sat back in her chair thinking that the party, after all, had been a great success. She had been well fed, had managed to say hello to everyone she was supposed to, and was almost ready to call it a night.

But just then a roll of the drums from the far end of the room announced the beginning of the after-dinner dancing, and when Roger and Gail stood up from the table, Gwen felt a hand on her shoulder. She turned to face Charles.

"May I have the pleasure of the first dance?" he asked, and although she groaned inwardly, she accepted his invitation. The band went into a long, energetic series of numbers from waltzes to disco, and Gwen found herself in the arms of one partner after another. She finally gave herself up to the music and decided that she would let go and have fun, and would try to forget all about her problems at Tonkan.

She was amused by the variety of her partners, many of whom she had never seen at work. But there in the background, always lurking close by, was the figure of Charles Norman. When he came back repeatedly for more dances, she felt more and more uneasy, but she still couldn't bring herself to refuse him. This is the last one, she told herself, and accepted his offer of a waltz.

"Did I already tell you how lovely you look

tonight, Gwen?" Charles asked as he pulled her closely to him.

"Thank you," she responded formally, and instinctively stiffened her body a little in an effort to maintain the distance between them.

"That purple really suits you." He looked down at her dress, in a way that made her wish that the bodice weren't quite so low.

Just relax, she told herself when the band went immediately into another slow number. It's your own fault for consenting to dance with him in the first place. You'll have to suffer the consequences and somehow get through it.

"I've been thinking a lot about you," he said finally after steering her into a corner of the room where there were fewer people. "A beautiful woman like you should go far at Tonkan." The insinuation behind his words alarmed her, and she bristled instinctively.

"I'm not quite sure I know what you mean," Gwen said, and tried, in vain, to pull herself away.

"I mean that it's quite unusual for a woman who is so intelligent, who has so much talent, to also be as beautiful as you." He leaned over and brought his cheek down against hers, and was now talking in low tones, directly into her ear. "We company boys like beautiful women, you know. With a little cooperation, you could go a long way. . . ."

"I don't know what you're talking about," she said, and began an active struggle to free herself. His hot breath on her face and his suffocating nearness was putting her on the edge of hysteria.

"Don't play dumb with me," he said. There

was an edge of cruelty in his voice. "You know exactly what I'm talking about." His hand snaked from her waist to the tip of her hips as his greedy eyes lunged for a taste of her breasts.

Gwen felt something close to hatred for this presumptuous man and hoped she would not have to risk making a scene in order to get away. "I'm sorry, Charles." She decided that she would try and be civil. "I'm suddenly not feeling well. I wonder if you would excuse me."

"Oh, come on," he whined, and she could see now that he was more than a little drunk. "Just finish this one dance." He lowered his lips to the crevice of her neck.

"No," she blurted out, and tried again to break away. She was beginning to feel faint, as if the room were closing in around her.

"May I cut in?" came a voice from nowhere, and Gwen was flooded with relief she had never known before. Her gratitude turned to surprise when she looked up and saw Kurt, tapping impatiently on Charles's shoulder.

"Come on, Charles," Kurt kidded him. "Don't be greedy. You've already had your turn."

Charles didn't give in easily, though, and it took some insisting on Kurt's part before he released her. Finally he relented, and Gwen could feel the tenseness leave her body as she stepped into the circle of Kurt's arms. It was like coming home.

They danced together for a while in silence, and Gwen took giant gulps of air in an effort to collect herself and calm her rapid heartbeat. She was not helped by the fact that, as her fear dissipated, it

was replaced by a different kind of excitement,
the kind Kurt had always ignited in her. Finally,
when she felt more or less in control again, she
looked up at Kurt and said, "Thanks. You really
saved me this time."

"I could see that," he responded seriously. "Are
you okay, Gwen?"

"Yes . . . I mean no. I'm not okay, really. I
think it's going to take me a little while to recover
from this little encounter."

Kurt gave her a long, inquisitive look, as if he
didn't quite understand and wanted to think for a
moment. How could she tell him that Charles
Norman had as much as offered her free reign at
Tonkan if she would sleep with him and the rest
of his cronies.

The music stopped but Kurt didn't release her,
and Gwen made no effort to step out of his supportive embrace. The orchestra went into a slow
waltz, and Kurt began to lead her in a series of
turns across the floor. The song was sweet, melodic,
and she felt herself move with the gentle, beat.
Finally, she was starting to relax and allowed her
eyes to close. The dark world of the sensuous
music was the safest place for her to go now.
There would be no trouble there, she was sure.
Kurt, her friend, would protect her.

"What right does he think he has, pawing you
like that?" Gwen was jarred back to reality by
Kurt's sudden eruption.

"You'd be surprised," she answered, and all of
her resentment came flooding back. The music
had offered her a false escape. She could neither
change nor forget what had happened, and she

felt almost dirty because of it. As if she had encouraged Charles, and was partly responsible.

"He actually thinks you'd go to bed with him?" Kurt asked. Gwen could see that he was fumbling his way to the truth, a certainty, she could see, that left him shocked and angry.

"Of course." She would be straight with him. "It's the price he feels I ought to pay for my job at Tonkan."

Kurt clenched his jaw in response to her reply, and for a moment Gwen was afraid. She could see that he was extremely angry, and she didn't want the situation to get out of hand.

Kurt said nothing more but instead led her toward the edge of the crowd, in the direction of the balcony just off the dance floor. "You don't mind stepping outside?" he asked. "I'd like to talk to you."

"No," said Gwen, thinking that she could use a little air.

Outside he steered her to the edge of the balcony. He leaned over the railing and stared out into space for a long moment. She appreciated the silence, and let the soft evening breeze flutter through her hair and cool her flushed cheeks. The slight wind offered relief, both physical and emotional, and teased her back into a state of calm.

Kurt seemed to sense that she had finally found her equilibrium and turned to speak to her. "Gwen, you may not appreciate this question, but I have to ask it. Was there any reason for Norman to think that he might have had a chance to get anywhere with you?"

"Are you out of your mind?" Gwen responded, horrified that he would think such a thing. "Are you asking me if I led him on . . . if I actually encouraged him to try and seduce me?"

"I'm sorry, Gwen," Kurt apologized whole-heartedly for his lack of trust. "After my long diatribe in Mexico about Angie, you'd think I'd be more aware of the sexual blackmail that goes on behind the scenes. It's just that I never dreamed it could happen to you . . . that Norman would actually believe that a woman of your caliber would be interested in that kind of a deal. The reason for my stupid question . . ."

Gwen waited patiently for Kurt to continue, but he stood motionless, silently brooding as he stared out into the dark night. Suddenly he began to beat the railing with a clenched fist. He whirled around to face the door and with a set chin declared, "I've got half a notion to go back in there and tell that slob just exactly—"

"Kurt, no!" Gwen implored him. She reached up and put her hand on his elbow in what she feared would be a futile attempt to detain him. "Please don't. For my sake. Please don't make a scene."

He looked down at her and said nothing. But she could tell from the softening of his expression that she had gotten through to him. "You're right," he said, relenting. He turned back to lean over the railing after moving slightly closer to her.

"Thank you." Gwen sighed her relief. "I do appreciate your tact."

Kurt accepted the compliment with a virtuous grin. "But I promise you that one way or another,

I'm going to let that loser know exactly what I think of him. And that if I had anything to say about it, if he ever tries anything like this again, the entire Tonkan staff is going to know about it."

"I suspect that he will try it again," Gwen said, "but you can be sure that he'll never come near me. And that if he ever tries, he's going to be very sorry."

"You've convinced me," Kurt said, and gave her a tight I'm-proud-of-you hug. She flashed back a grateful smile.

"You know what?" she said after a moment's thought. "I just realized that Charles probably thinks he's so attractive that any woman would jump at the chance to sleep with him." She giggled at the absurdity of her theory. He was, she thought, such a grossly undesirable man.

"Oh, I'm sure he probably thinks he's Tonkan's answer to Erroll Flynn," Kurt said dramatically, and Gwen laughed. "But even if he were, it wouldn't matter. What he did was wrong, and makes me suspicious about the character of all those chauvinists who are running Tonkan."

Her eyebrows arched in surprise. Chauvinists? Had Kurt actually used that word?

He noticed her surprise and leaned forward a little so that his elbow expanded and came to rest against her arm. "Surprised, aren't you?" He couldn't help but grin. "I guess I have to admit that I know the meaning of the word through firsthand experience, Gwen. And you're partially responsible for helping me realize it."

She was all too conscious of his touch on her arm and wondered if she should move away. She tried to concentrate on what he was saying, but the words were lost in the memories his touch conjured up.

Gwen looked up into Kurt's serious, handsome face that was half lit in the gilded moonlight. The thick clouds that had shaded the moon had now drifted aside so that the light from the golden orb lit up the heavens and sent golden arrows shooting across the sapphire sky.

"When I think back on my attitude toward you when you first came to Tonkan, I feel almost ashamed of myself, Gwen." The gravity of his expression called for her full attention. "I have to admit that I was probably even thinking along the lines of Charles Norman then. I guess I came to realize it when you started getting on my case about Connie."

Ah yes, Connie, Gwen thought, and what was the beginning of a heady mood turned to cool sobriety.

"It all started out as kind of an experiment, my giving Connie more responsibility, just to see how she would do. I was shocked when I saw how I had underrated her. And to think I had been impressed by her fast typing." He flashed her a somewhat guilty smile.

"Three cheers for you," Gwen said earnestly, and shivered under the next, cooler gust of wind.

"Are you cold?" Kurt asked.

"Just a little," she said quietly.

He put a protective arm around her shoulders and turning her toward him said, "Let's go down to the end of the balcony where there's a little less breeze."

His arm slid to her waist as they walked, and she fell into step beside him in perfect synchronization. She felt as if they had been walking together, side by side, for years, or maybe even for a lifetime.

He led her to the bench and she sat down in languid resignation, warning her hungry body not to be alarmed and not to expect anyting from the mere closeness of him. She was alone now, she told herself. Kurt was already taken. He would undoubtedly come to be a good friend. But that was where the relationship ended.

"Once I saw how badly I was treating Connie," he reiterated, "I came to my senses and actually began taking an interest in her career."

Gwen turned to look at the man beside her, the man so different now from the person she once knew. His face was so close that if she moved forward, just a little, she could almost touch it.

"I'm proud of you," she said finally, and then added, "and since Connie's not the only woman working with you, I assume the rest of us are also going to benefit from the change."

"Of course," Kurt said, but didn't go on.

Gwen was pensive for a moment, trying to decide whether or not she should cater to her curiosity about exactly what had happened. Finally her inquisitive nature got the better of her, and she asked, "But Kurt, I'm really curious about something. How exactly was Connie able to bring you around so quickly?"

He seemed surprised by the question, and Gwen thought she had made a mistake in getting so personal. He rubbed his hand across his chin as if he was thinking. Finally he said, "I guess it's a case of actions speaking louder than words. Connie simply went ahead and did her job—and did it extremely well—without even mentioning the fact that I was piling enough work on her for two people. One day *I* was so backed up with work that I asked her to write the summation report of a contract that had just been negotiated. I read it at the next meeting and realized that it was very good. After the meeting several people came up to congratulate me not only on the contract but also on the presentation. It was then that it hit me that Connie was the sole author of the thing—and that the write-up was, in many ways, even more effective than what I could have done myself."

"Interesting." Gwen tried to sound sincere, but inside she couldn't help but wonder about the blow it must have dealt to his ego.

"The next day I didn't say anything to her other than to thank her and to compliment her on her work. But from then on, believe me, I kept my eye on her. You know, Gwen," he said as he slid his arm along the back of the bench and accidentally brushed a thumb across her bare shoulders, "I think Connie probably had it all figured out by then. Somehow, even though we hadn't actually discussed what was going on, she managed to not only illuminate me as to the superior quality of her work, but also made it clear that my attitude to her was patronizing and, to use that word again, chauvinistic."

Gwen looked at Kurt, her eyes wide with interest. She had never dreamed that she would be hearing him talk like this. She squirmed a little in an attempt to put a little more distance between them, all too aware of her contact with his hand as it rested against the back of her neck.

"The odd part of it all was that neither of us said anything about what was going on," he continued with a slight grin. "Then one morning after we had both settled down to work, I made the coffee and asked her if she wanted a cup. I served it to her the same way she served me in the good old days. The irony of the situation struck us both at the same time, and we started to laugh. I'll never forget that moment, Gwen. It was the beginning of my change in outlook. A change that was mostly due to you."

"It's a wonderful story, Kurt," Gwen said honestly. "But I'm not so sure how much I actually had to do with it. After all, we really haven't seen very much of one another since we got back from Mexico."

She felt his body stiffen and realized that she had said the one word that he probably didn't want to hear. Mexico. The scene of so much torment for both of them.

"Yes, Mexico . . ." He seemed to be thinking back on it all, and she saw his expression change from one of contentment to what looked like deep meloncholy. "I guess you and I weren't as lucky as Connie and I have been. Somehow, we never did manage to work out our disagreements. . . ."

Gwen tried to swallow the sad sigh that nearly escaped her lips, knowing that in this case he wasn't only referring to their business relationship.

"But then"—his voice became even more solemn—"I think that one of the problems was that we never took the time to talk. Things moved so fast—and when we hit a snag we slammed the doors too quickly, and too hard.''

"I know," she whispered. But she couldn't hold back a surge of anger both at herself and at Kurt when she thought about how they had put off addressing their misunderstandings and had somehow thought they would be solved by making love.

"You may not believe this, Gwen." Kurt turned to face her, and she felt obliged to meet his serious, dark eyes. "But I've been trying to talk to you ever since we've been back. I realized, for one thing, what a fool I was to respond the way I did to your promotion. I should have apologized for that long ago. But I knew that I would have to pay the price of waiting until things settled down a little before I could even hope we could talk about what happened in Mexico."

"Oh?" Gwen said, "I thought we did that in the cab. After all, look how well we've managed to work together."

"Don't tell me that you didn't know I wanted to straighten things out," he said, angered by her passive response. "You know damn well that you've been avoiding me like the plague ever since we've been back. The only time I've had a chance to talk with you has been at work, and of course, *everything* that goes on at Tonkan is strictly business."

"I just thought it was better if we kept our distance," she said. "Especially after what's happened between you and Connie."

"This has nothing at all to do with me and

Connie," Kurt said loudly. The orchestra was still going full tilt, and its soft, velvety strains wafted out the balcony door and clashed with the sound of Kurt's brash voice.

Gwen silently admonished herself for mixing the private and professional aspects of their lives. Of course Connie and Kurt's romantic involvement had nothing to do with his attempt at putting their business relationship back into order. "I guess a lot of it has been my fault, Kurt," she said. "I've just been slower than you in coming to see the full value of our collaboration at Tonkan." *And it's taken me longer to fall out of love with you,* her inner voice of truth added its note of despair.

Gwen felt as if the tense conversation was draining her of what little emotional stamina she had left after her confrontation with Charles. When she lifted her head and looked up at the stars, she saw that the once-brilliant sky now looked flat. Its millions of flickering lights seemed veiled by a dark cloud of defeat, as if the night had suddenly lost its magic and had become just another, ordinary evening.

Kurt withdrew his arm from the back of the bench and sat looking down at his folded hands. Gwen had a feeling that he had forgotten that she was there, sitting so close beside him but, in truth, at such a distance.

"Why don't we arrange to have lunch together one day next week and see what we can do about improving our working relationship?" she suggested, hoping that Kurt wouldn't recognize the false enthusiasm in her voice. She sat back and tried to convince herself that her suggestion was generous, and surely the most rational thing to do.

There was a long pause before he finally looked at her and said, "I guess you're right, Gwen. At this point, we might as well put some effort into our working relationship and do what's best for Tonkan. I promise to make as much effort with you as I have with Connie," he said somewhat insensitively, and she barely managed to hide the grimace that flashed across her face. He stood up then and, taking her hand in his, pulled her up alongside of him. "Maybe someday soon we can think about tackling a friendship again," he said in a voice that was thick with resignation. "For now, I guess all we can be is fellow saplings amongst the dead wood."

Gwen knew he was trying to lighten the situation, but somehow she didn't feel like laughing.

Chapter Eleven

❧

"I don't care what you say, Gwen, I'm not going to let you go to work with a temperature of 101."

"But Betty. I've got so much to do. . . ." Gwen croaked back in protest. Her raw throat stung painfully when she tried to talk, bringing tears to the corners of her glassy eyes.

"I don't know what you picked up, but it's nothing to take lightly. If you stay in bed today, maybe you can shake it. I only wish I could afford to skip a couple of classes so you'd have someone here with you."

"Oh, Betty, don't be silly," Gwen said. "It's one thing for me to take a sick day, and an entirely different matter for you to take off, too, just to keep me company. But I guess you're right," she said resignedly as a cold chill rippled through her body. She pulled the comforter up under her chin. "I should stay home and try to get well. Thank God I've got a good assistant who knows how to handle things. As a matter of fact, maybe I can arrange to have someone drop some work off, so the day won't be a total waste."

"I give up!" Betty flung her hands into the air. "I have never in my life seen anyone more addicted to her work than you. I swear, sometimes I wonder if you aren't becoming an outright fanatic." She laughed.

Gwen tried to laugh back at her, but winced in pain when she triggered another tickle in her sore throat.

"I'm going to make you a quick cup of tea before I leave," said Betty as she brought the phone over to the bed. "Why don't you call Tonkan and tell them you're not coming in."

Gwen dialed Tonkan and within seconds had reported her condition to her assistant, Naomi, and had instructed her to gather together several of the more urgent files and send them to her either by messenger or with someone from Tonkan who might be going her way. It wouldn't matter if she got them in the afternoon; she would probably be feeling better by then and would have a chance to work that evening.

Just then Betty reentered the room carrying a cup of steaming tea in one hand and a newspaper in the other. "Just as I suspected," she said, holding up the newspaper for Gwen to see, and read the headlines that said, SEVERE FLUE BUG HITS STATE. "You probably picked it up at that office brawl Saturday night. You were out awfully late," she said kiddingly, and shook her finger at her friend.

"I only wish it had been for a better reason," said Gwen, thinking back on how unsatisfied she had felt after she left Kurt that evening, as if somehow, even after their conversation, something had not been resolved.

"Well, I've got to run." Betty jumped up in her usual, energetic manner. "Now you take good care of yourself today. Stay in bed and get plenty of rest."

Gwen smiled at her friend's attempt at playing doctor. "Thanks, Betty," she said gratefully, and then sank back into the soft pillows. She took a sip of the hot tea and had a hard time swallowing. So she reached over, set her cup down on the nightstand beside the bed and, pulling herself fully under the pile of blankets that Betty had heaped on the bed, slipped into a sound sleep.

Three hours later, she awoke with a start. For a moment she felt disoriented, as if she couldn't quite remember what she was doing there. She rubbed her smarting eyes and gulped for a breath of air. Oh yes, she thought, she had the flu and had been sleeping. . . . She supposed it was the gnawing feeling of hunger in her stomach that had woken her up. As she flung the covers off to the side and slipped into her warm yellow robe she smiled at the realization that only the most dire trauma ever seemed to interfere with her always hearty appetite.

Once in the kitchen, Gwen poured a generous portion of tasty minestrone soup into a saucepan and stood over it until it began to boil. Then she sat down at the table and quickly began to eat. Her throat felt better now, and her temperature seemed to have gone down a bit. After finishing her soup and preparing another mug of tea with lemon, she started back to bed, knowing that sleep was, in the end, the best cure for her illness.

But a new restlessness seemed to have replaced the heavy cloud of grogginess that had hung over her in the morning. She had just decided that she would make one more attempt to fall asleep again when she heard the doorbell ring. It's probably the messenger from Tonkan, she thought. She grabbed for her robe and, after untying a few snarls of hair with her fingers in an effort to repair her state of disarray, walked quickly to the door.

"You shouldn't be out of bed!" a deep male voice roared at her even before it was open.

"Kurt!" she gasped. "What are *you* doing here?"

"Someone said you needed these." He pointed to the files he had tucked under his arm. "I happened to be coming this way anyway, so I volunteered to drop them off."

"Oh," Gwen muttered, still shocked at seeing him. "Would you like to come in? But I warn you, I'm probably contagious."

"It doesn't matter," he said confidently. "I never get sick. And even if I did"—he grinned down at her—"I'd probably enjoy the time off."

"I wish I did," Gwen admitted, and then realized that she had been standing in a draft. An involuntary shiver passed through her body and she folded her arms across her chest.

"Hey," said Kurt, suddenly alarmed. "I saw that. What *are* you doing out of bed?"

"I guess you're right." She acquiesced without a struggle. There was something very satisfying about placing herself in his care.

"Now, what can I get you?" he asked as he tucked the covers up under her chin. Gwen wiggled and squirmed until she had loosened them enough to extract her arms, then sat up.

"I really don't think I need anything," she said

as she picked up her cup of tea. "If I were well I'd offer to make you one."

"I think that would hit the spot," Kurt said as he stood up. Gwen noticed that he was wearing a casual, light brown suit that she hadn't seen before. His handsome, tidy appearance made her realize how frumpy she must look, and when he went to the kitchen to make his tea, she snuck out of bed long enough to pull a brush through her knotted hair.

"To your health," Kurt kidded when he returned, and raised his cup into the air before taking a swallow. He sat on the edge of the bed, so close that Gwen couldn't avoid his soft, mahogany eyes that were alight with warmth and concern.

"You didn't have to come," she began, not knowing exactly what to say.

"I wanted to, Gwen," he said, and then moved even closer. It was as if he wanted to make sure she believed him before he went on. "First of all, I was worried about you," he said softly, "and secondly, I didn't like the way our conversation ended the other night. I knew that since you were sick in bed, I'd have you pinned down and you couldn't run out on me. What better chance to tell you what's really on my mind?" His words were light, but his tone was deadly serious.

He reached for her long, delicate fingers and trapped them within the warm, tight grasp of his hand. "After I dropped you off the other night and I thought back on our conversation, I couldn't as usual, make sense of anything that was said," he began. "It seemed as if it began all right, and that I was slowly fumbling my way toward what I really wanted to say to you, but as always, I got detoured, and wound up saying absolutely nothing.

"When I got home," he went on, "I remembered our spouting things like 'maybe we can get together some day,' and 'perhaps we can think about improving our collaboration.' It was then that I realized that the entire conversation had been absurd. After all that we had been through together, we were addressing one another like total strangers."

"Yes," Gwen said quietly. "It bothered me, too." A ripple of remorse coursed through her, and she lowered her eyes.

"Seriously, Gwen," Kurt said with a new wave of conviction, "I know that this is probably the worst time to be here, when you're feeling sick. But if you think you're strong enough, I'd really like to go on."

"I'm okay," she assured him. Though she was slightly weak, she could almost feel the relief that a candid conversation with Kurt would undoubtedly bring.

"I thought you handled Norman beautifully the other night," he said sincerely, "and I'm glad you stopped me from losing my temper. But it wasn't just that I was so furious over what he did, or that I equated it with my lousy experience with Angela. I was upset because he had dared try something with *you*, Gwen, and in all honesty, I know that I wouldn't have been nearly as outraged if it had been someone else."

Gwen offered him a weak smile of thanks. Having once been her lover, she supposed that it was natural for him to have a strong reaction to

Charles's abusive behavior. In the pause that followed, she instinctively reached up to touch the bow at the neckline of her nightgown, making sure it was still tied. She remembered, suddenly, that the flimsy gown wasn't exactly modest. But she didn't dare check to see if she was fully covered. Not while Kurt was sitting so close, pinning her down with his alert eyes that refused to miss anything.

He lifted her cup from off the nightstand and put it into her hands. "Drink more," he ordered, and she immediately raised the now lukewarm liquid to her lips. Before he went on, he also took a swallow from his own cup. "I remembered, too, that ridiculous comment about the advantages of our becoming close colleagues, and how it would benefit Tonkan." He shook his head from side to side in disbelief. "I knew that there was a lot of distance between us, but to give it all up and decide to work on a relationship that was molded to suit Tonkan seemed crazy. It was then that I started thinking back over the last few months, and still couldn't come up with the right answer to the question that's been plaguing me for weeks. Gwen," he said earnestly, and set down his cup again, "what exactly did I do to make you dislike me so?"

"What?" she asked incredulously. The question had taken her by surprise and in fact she wasn't sure she even understood it. . . .

"I've barely been able to get near you at the office," he explained after seeing her confusion. "You've made it perfectly clear that you have no interest in coming anywhere near me," he went on. "I know I acted badly when you got your promotion, but I was still unaware of a lot of things then. After I finally got things straightened out with Connie, I realized how insulting my little show of jealousy had been. But I couldn't get near you to apologize," he said helplessly.

Gwen noticed how stuffy the room had become and felt as if she was having a hard time breathing. She let the covers slip down to encircle her waist, not caring anymore about her modesty. She knew that the answer to his question was Connie. But if she told him how she felt about Connie, she would have to admit that she was jealous of her; she would have to admit that she couldn't stand seeing him with another woman. And that would be admitting that she still cared. . . .

"I'm not quite sure why I avoided you, Kurt," she said evasively. "After all, Mexico *was* a thing of the past, and you were so helpful when I started my new job."

One glance and she could tell that he didn't believe her. He pulled himself up further on the bed and, leaning across her outstretched legs, propped himself up with one elbow. He didn't have to say anything for her to know that he wasn't satisfied with her explanation and that he would sit there until she gave him a straight answer.

Gwen raised her hand to muffle a cough and tried to stall for time. Finally she said in a trembling voice, "It was just that when you and Connie got together . . ." Her mind went blank, and she couldn't go on.

"What about me and Connie?" Kurt demanded an answer.

After a moment, she said, "At first I was upset when I realized that the two of you had become so close. I guess that I was actually a little bit jealous. But I think I've come around, slowly, and that I can accept it now. I really do hope you and Connie will be very happy, Kurt."

"You sound as if you're giving us your blessing," he roared at her, and pulled himself a little away.

"Well, you're both my friends, and I wanted you to know that I wouldn't—that is that what happened between us shouldn't—well, that I wouldn't mind if you and Connie—not that it matters if I mind—" She knew she wasn't making sense, but she was frightened by the black scowl that darkened his face.

"You know, Gwen, for a smart woman you can be pretty obtuse at times." He stood up and began pacing from the foot of the bed over to the window and then back again.

"Thanks!" She was shocked by the sudden insult.

"Where on earth did you get the idea that I'm seeing Connie?" he shouted at her.

"I don't know," Gwen stammered. She had to admit that her information had come through hearsay, that neither one of them had actually come to her and told her that they were involved.

She looked up at Kurt through thick, dark lashes. She saw a rigid, angry man, pacing the floor, and the force of his fury gave her a chill. He had found the last piece in a difficult puzzle, a piece that had, ironically, destroyed the entire picture.

"Kurt, I . . ." Gwen tried to talk, tried to break through to him and apologize for the misunderstanding.

"Well, I must say," he interrupted her, "this certainly does explain a lot. He walked over to the edge of the bed. "For your information"—he looked down at her through eyes that smarted with accusation—"there's never been anything between Connie and me. Except for the fact that we've developed one of the best friendships I've ever had with a woman."

Under the gun of his intense stare, Gwen felt vulnerable and looked back at him with a combination of guilt and resentment. That last remark had been cruel, she thought, meant to punish her for her mistake. She raised a hand to her forehead and wiped at the tiny beads of perspiration that hung, like pearls, from temple to temple. No fever now, she thought frantically, trying subconsciously to extricate herself from the painful scene. She felt cold, as if all the initial warmth that Kurt had offered her had suddenly turned to ice.

"Cover up," he said impatiently, and leaned down to pull the blankets up under her chin. "You'll catch pneumonia!" His steely voice indicated the extent of his anger. Suddenly he grabbed for her teacup and turned toward the door, saying, "I'm going to make you another cup of tea before I leave."

"Don't bother," she whispered after him, too late. When he left the room, she found that she was flooded by contradictory feelings about what had happened. A part of her felt as if she couldn't live through another separation from Kurt. I still love him, she thought, as hot tears fell down her cheeks and spotted the pink, floral sheet that was drawn up around her.

"Here you are." Kurt walked briskly back into the room. He set the steaming cup down and, looking at her for a last time, said, "I'm sorry, Gwen. It's hard for me to believe that you would trust me so little that you would think I had started something with Connie . . . so soon after what happened in Mexico."

He sounded so genuinely hurt, so betrayed, that she felt her eyes once more fill with tears.

"Take care of yourself," he said as he walked to the door. "I know the way out. . . ."

Gwen felt in that moment that her heart had broken. She tried desperately to hold back her sobs until she heard the click of the latch and knew that Kurt was out the door and out of her life for good. Unconsciously, she held her breath, and waited for what seemed a long time. But all she could hear was the racing of her own pulse and the escalating drone of her own heartbeat.

Finally she thought she heard the door close, and she was just about to give in to her emotions when Kurt's deep voice came wafting back inside her room. "No!" she heard him declare, and then his footsteps, growing louder as he approached her room. When she dared look up, he was once more standing over her.

"I'm not going to make the same mistake again," he said resolutely. He stared down at her for a long time, and she could see the tension in his face slowly melt away. Now he was taking a care-ful survey of her, from the top of her head to the amorphous lump under the covers that was her feet. "I'm not going to go without saying what I came here to say," he announced firmly, and once again he sat down beside her. His entire body had begun to relax now, and Gwen saw a new wave of tenderness wash over him and break through his earlier rage.

"Gwen." He reached over and took her hand. He held it in his own as if it were a piece of art, and his own palm the pedestal. "Do you remember when we were in Mexico and you told me a little bit about your family?"

"Yes," she said, and thought back on the scene that now seemed as if it had taken place years ago.

As he spoke he carefully examined each one of her fingers. "I didn't tell you then how affected I was by your story, how moved I was when I saw the deep love that you must have felt for your parents. And the respect that seemed to go with it."

He waited for a moment, as if he wanted to let the full impact of what he was telling her sink in. And, Gwen suspected, it couldn't be very easy to reveal what he was about to say.

"I was also," he finally began again, "jealous. I compared it to my own sterile upbringing. I don't want to bore you with a lengthy diatribe about my life, Gwen, but I think that a short explanation of my childhood will help explain my behavior.

"Almost every word you used to describe your family life was the exact opposite of what I could say about mine. Yours was warm, mine was cold. Yours was secure, and mine was insecure. You were poor as a child, and I never for a moment had to worry about not having enough money. It's kind of interesting, isn't it?" he asked a bit cynically as he lowered her hand to the bed. "We represent the results of two very different kinds of families. You'd think that you and I would be as different as night from day. . . ."

Almost without knowing it, Gwen turned her hand so that she was gripping his, trying to show him that she understood what he had missed and would be willing to do anything to share what she had had with him.

"I guess I never told you that I was from Michigan. The son of a wealthy businessman. Automotive." Kurt began to fill in the picture, and Gwen sat quietly, listening intently. "Dad was a nice enough guy I guess, and probably started out as a real human being, just like everyone else. But by the time he was a young man he was addicted to the buck, even though he had inherited enough to get by on for the rest of his life.

"And, of course when your goal is to pile high your gold and climb the proverbial social ladder so you can show off your riches, you naturally marry someone like my mother, the darling of the social circle. Thinking back on it, they probably made a pretty good couple. Neither one of them gave a damn about anything but power and money, so neither felt any lack of affection. The first time she got pregnant, with my brother, Stan, it had all been planned. By the time he was born she had all her nannies and nurses lined up so that she didn't have to lift a finger. It seems that they were quite delighted with Stan, as he turned out to be a very obedient child who took to their world like a duck to water. Ah, and Stan was smart, too, and a shining star all the way through school. He seemed to breeze along through life, happy as a clam with his high test scores and his parents' approval."

Kurt stopped for a moment to catch his breath. Gwen felt that he was getting to the point of his entrance into the story, and intuition told her that it wasn't going to be easy.

"Am I tiring you?" he asked, and when she shook her head no he continued. "When Stan was about seven, my parents, one night, had an accident—me. My mother never let me forget the good times she gave up carrying me.

"Oh, my upbringing from the start was more or less like Stan's—except that it was a little more solitary. I guess everyone else was out working or social climbing or something.

"Luckily, school always came easy, and I saw it as a chance to prove to my mother that her accident hadn't turned out all bad. But it didn't work—my parents expected good grades, they didn't reward them. The one that it really seemed to affect was Stan. He developed a fiercely competitive attitude toward me as soon as he saw me succeeding. And although I didn't initially want to compete with him, if I am that way now, I learned it from trying to get back at Stan."

"Oh," Gwen said sadly, trying to conceal the real pain she felt for him.

"I left home eventually, and came to Minnesota, and at one point or another really did become interested in computers. And to make a long story short, here I am, an ever-faithful employee of Tonkan."

"And your parents?" Gwen was almost afraid to ask.

"I write to my mother every now and then. Father died five years ago," Kurt said with no show of remorse.

He turned slightly and, taking a deep breath of air, said, "Now that you know the background, I might as well get to the point of it all. Gwen, it's possible that I've never loved anyone in my life, not really. Oh, I've managed to construct a rather charming personality, and I've developed the capacity for affection. And there certainly have been no problems finding women. Somehow I've managed to keep them at just the right distance to be comfortable. . . ."

What was this all leading up to? Gwen wondered.

"But *you*. You seemed different from the day I met you. Then, when we finally got together in Mexico, I experienced a feeling I never had before. I fell head over heels in love with you. I can honestly tell you that at first it was damned uncomfortable," he said with a little smile, "until I realized it was love. Then I was thrilled. My only mistake was in not convincing you of it. And, of course, letting my competitiveness get the better of me. . . ." His voice was filled with defeat.

"Oh, Kurt," Gwen cried, and choked back her tears. Was it possible that what he was saying was true?

He raised her fingers to his lips and offered each one a gentle kiss. "When we got back from Mexico, I knew I had been a fool to take it for granted that you would marry me—and even give up your work. But I still thought we could straighten things out between us, that I could make you forgive me for my ridiculous behavior."

Gwen reached out again and this time held on to his arm. Inside she felt the rumblings of a huge celebration. *Kurt loves me* kept ringing through her ears, and she felt strong, jubilant, and free of every anxiety she had ever known.

"I was terrified that you would take the job with Phanor, and that somehow we would get separated, and that I would never find you again. And throughout it all," he said earnestly, as if he was finally getting to the core of his feelings, "I was constantly worried that I might love you too much. You see, I was a master at casual relationships but a total novice when it came to the real thing. You had become the sole source of all of my happiness, and I was getting to the point where I was sure that I couldn't live without you. It scared me, Gwen"—he brushed his thumb across her cheek—"not knowing for sure how you felt about me."

Gwen reached up and pressed his palm to her lips. "Oh, darling. Don't blame yourself. I've put so much stock in my career, wanted so much to be a success and impress I-don't-know-who, that I did lose sight of other, more important things. I shoved aside all of my feelings for you when I thought there was a possibility I might be hurt—or when I felt I might have to compromise my position a little." She sighed deeply and held on tightly to Kurt's hand. It wasn't easy, this confession.

"But deep down I knew all along that I loved

you, too. I knew that I wanted you from the moment I met you, and that, in the end, I would have to have you. I love you, Kurt," she whispered as she peered into the shimmering depths of his eyes that were, like her own, moist from tears of joy.

He bent down and in one sudden motion pulled her up and into his arms. He held her face steady with one hand and brought his lips down hard on her mouth.

"Kurt!" she moaned, and beat gently on his back with her fists. "I'm sick!"

"I know," he said, and gave her a broad smile. He reached out and pulled on the end of the bow until it came undone and the neck of her nightgown fell open.

"Kurt," Gwen insisted. "I'm contagious. You'll get the flu."

"Good," he said, looking happier than she had ever seen him. "That'll mean that the two patients will just have to stay in bed for a couple of days—together."

He pushed aside her nightgown to kiss the hollow of her throat, and slowly her protestations began to subside. His strong hands reached up and under her nightgown and began to stroke her back and shoulders, and she gave in to the rapture that was bubbling up inside of her.

For a moment Kurt let go of Gwen and quickly shrugged off his coat jacket. Then he lay down beside her and pulled her down next to him. "I love you, Gwen," he kept repeating against her hair, and then, "I'll always be with you."

The sound of his voice soothed her. At last she

had found love, the one ingredient that had been missing for so long.

Kurt let his hand slide down across her neck to her full breasts and teased their rosy tips until they sprang out in anticipation of the warmth of his mouth and teasing tongue. Her breath quickened, and she gasped as he stroked her smooth, flat stomach and made his way further down until he parted her thighs and found the warm center of her desire.

Gwen's eager body arched toward him, and she let her lips track their own path of kisses across his broad, muscular chest. She yanked impatiently at his shirt, demanding that it be discarded with the rest of his clothing. He obliged, then turned to her, removed her nightgown, and turned back the bedding so that they would have no further obstacles between them. All of her senses were perfectly tuned to receive everything he had to offer her. Her deep thirst for him had never been stronger, and now that it was finally about to be assuaged, she realized the full extent of her need. "Kurt." She whispered his name ardently and strained toward him. But he held her back for a moment, as if wanting to take one last look at his lover before they set out together on the mad journey to the heart of their passion, where there was water to quench their thirst and love to heal their bruises and strengthen their souls.

"I feel as if I'm making love to you for the first time," Kurt murmured as his hand slipped down onto her shapely thigh. "But before we do," he said very seriously, "I'm asking you—will you marry me?"

"Yes, oh yes," Gwen said, and with that her happiness was complete. Their lovemaking tonight would be more special, more precious than anything either of them had ever felt before, because they were in love, and they had the rest of their lives to explore love together.

The moment they came together, Gwen felt as if she were being carried far, far away from her familiar reality into a dream world that she'd never known existed. Now she and Kurt were strolling together, hand in hand, in a beautiful, exotic garden of sensual delights where their ravenous appetites and deep needs would finally be fulfilled. The sun shone down in shiny, golden rays that warmed their naked bodies and brought a rosy flush to their flailing limbs.

Tiny drops of dew hung on the grass and provided a soft, moist carpet under their tender feet, and long, wispy green vines wrapped themselves like ribbons around the trees and formed an elegant archway overhead. The lovers dined, first daintily and then voraciously, on the tart juice of the plump, ripe fruit that seemed to grow everywhere. Then they drank from gourds of ruby-red wine, until they were drunk from the rich love potion. Gwen's soft, open mouth found Kurt's lips, the headiest brew.

At last they approached the crest of their happiness, the summit of their journey. They locked more tightly together, and Kurt groaned in pleasure. Then he cried out her name in a savage growl, and the sound sent them spinning, spinning back to reality, and to a world where nothing would ever separate them again.

"Where am I?" Gwen asked in a soft drowsy voice as she blinked her eyes and looked around.

"Silly." Kurt laughed down at her and kissed the tip of her nose. "You fell asleep for a little while," he said softly, and cradled her more comfortably in his arms.

"Oh." She sighed, and curled her fingers around the back of his neck. "How long did I sleep?"

"Just a few minutes." He grinned down at her. He kissed her forehead, her neck, and the hollow in her shoulder.

"Kurt," she whimpered when she felt a ripple of desire pass through her. "We can't . . . I mean, we just . . ."

Kurt shot her a wicked smile just as the phone rang. Gwen reached up over her head and brought the receiver to her ear.

"Oh hi," she said as he began to examine her tiny, perfect foot. She giggled and slapped his hand away. "Yes, Betty, I'm feeling much better."

Kurt flung a muscular thigh up and across her stomach and lowered his mouth to her breast. "Definitely," Gwen announced to her friend, "I am on the road to recovery. . . ." At last, she thought, and turned back to him.

TELL US YOUR OPINIONS AND RECEIVE A FREE COPY OF THE RAPTURE NEWSLETTER.

Thank you for filling out our questionnaire. Your response to the following questions will help us to bring you more and better books. In appreciation of your help we will send you a free copy of the Rapture Newsletter.

1. Book Title:_____

   Book #:_____ (5-7)

2. Using the scale below how would you rate this book on the following features? Please write in one rating from 0-10 for each feature in the spaces provided. Ignore bracketed numbers.

(Poor) 0 1 2 3 4 5 6 7 8 9 10 (Excellent)

0-10 Rating

Overall Opinion of Book. . . . . _____ (8)
Plot/Story. . . . . _____ (9)
Setting/Location. . . . . _____ (10)
Writing Style. . . . . _____ (11)
Dialogue. . . . . _____ (12)
Love Scenes. . . . . _____ (13)
Character Development:
Heroine:. . . . . _____ (14)
Hero:. . . . . _____ (15)
Romantic Scene on Front Cover. . . . . _____ (16)
Back Cover Story Outline . . . . _____ (17)
First Page Excerpts. . . . . _____ (18)

3. What is your: Education: Age:_____(20-22)

   High School ( )1   4 Yrs. College ( )3
   2 Yrs. College ( )2   Post Grad   ( )4 (23)

4. Print Name:_____

   Address:_____

   City:_____State:_____Zip:_____

   Phone # (   )_____ (25)

Thank you for your time and effort. Please send to New American Library, Rapture Romance Research Department, 1633 Broadway, New York, NY 10019.

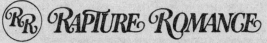

RAPTURE ROMANCE

*Provocative and sensual,
passionate and tender—
the magic and mystery of love
in all its many guises*

Coming next month

SEPTEMBER SONG by Lisa Moore. Swearing her career came first, Lauren Rose faced the challenge of her life in Mark Landrill's arms, for she had to choose between the work she thrived on—and a passion that left her both fulfilled and enslaved . . .

A MOUNTAIN MAN by Megan Ashe. For Kelly March, Josh Munroe's beloved mountain world was a haven where she could prove her independence. but Josh—who tormented her with desire—resented the intrusion. Could Kelly prove she was worth his love—and, if she did, would she lose all she'd fought to achieve?

THE KNAVE OF HEARTS by Estelle Edwards. Brilliant young lawyer Kate Sewell had no defense against carefree riverboat gambler Hal Lewis. But could Kate risk her career—even for the ecstasy his love promised?

BEYOND ALL STARS by Melinda McKenzie. For astronaut Ann Lafton, working with Commander Ed Saber brought emotional chaos that jeopardized their NASA shuttle mission. But Ann couldn't stop dreaming that this sensuous lover would fly her to the stars . . .

DREAMLOVER by JoAnn Robb. Painter K.L. Michaels needed Hunter St. James to pull off a daring masquerade, but she didn't count on losing her relaxed lifestyle as their wild love affair unfolded. Could their nights of sensual fireworks make up for their daily battles?

A LOVE SO FRESH by Marilyn Davids. Loving Ben Heron was everything Anna Markham needed. But she considered marriage a trap, and Ben, too, had been burned before. Passion drew them together, but was their rapture enough to overcome the obstacles they faced?

RAPTURE ROMANCE

Provocative and sensual, passionate and tender— the magic and mystery of love in all its many guises

New Titles Available Now

RAPTURE ROMANCE

Provocative and sensual, passionate and tender— the magic and mystery of love in all its many guises

RAPTURE ROMANCE

*Provocative and sensual,
passionate and tender—
the magic and mystery of love
in all its many guises*

Buy them at your local
bookstore or use coupon
on next page for ordering.

RAPTURE ROMANCE

Provocative and sensual,
passionate and tender—
the magic and mystery of love
in all its many guises

SPECIAL $1.00 REBATE OFFER
WHEN YOU BUY
FOUR RAPTURE ROMANCES

To receive your cash refund, send:

1. This coupon: To qualify for the $1.00 refund, this coupon, completed with your name and address, must be used. (Certificate may not be reproduced)

2. Proof of purchase: Print, on the reverse side of this coupon, the *title* of the books, the *numbers* of the books (on the upper right hand of the front cover preceding the price), and the U.P.C. numbers (on the back covers) on your next four purchases.

3. Cash register receipts, with prices circled to:
   Rapture Romance $1.00 Refund Offer
   P.O. Box NB037
   El Paso, Texas 79977

Offer good only in the U.S. and Canada. Limit one refund/response per household for any group of four Rapture Romance titles. Void where prohibited, taxed or restricted. Allow 6–8 weeks for delivery. Offer expires March 31, 1984.

NAME_____

ADDRESS_____

CITY_____STATE_____ZIP_____

SPECIAL $1.00 REBATE OFFER
WHEN YOU BUY
FOUR RAPTURE ROMANCES

See complete details on reverse

1. Book Title _____

Book Number 451-_____

U.P.C. Number 7116200195-_____

2. Book Title _____

Book Number 451-_____

U.P.C. Number 7116200195-_____

3. Book Title _____

Book Number 451-_____

U.P.C. Number 7116200195-_____

4. Book Title _____

Book Number 451-_____

U.P.C. Number 7116200195-_____

U.P.C. Number

0   SAMPLE

71162 00195